PULP
Literature

Pulp Literature Press
Issue No. 39, Summer 2023

Publisher: Pulp Literature Press; Editor-in-Chief: Jennifer Landels; Senior Editor: Mel Anastasiou; Acquisitions Editor: Genevieve Wynand; Poetry Editors: Daniel Cowper & Emily Osborne; Assistant Editors: Brooklynn Hook, Nik Kos, Jeya Thiessen, Sierra Louie, Ellen Spacey; Copy Editor: Amanda Bidnall; Proofreader: Sierra Louie; Graphic Design: Amanda Bidnall; Cover Design: Kate Landels; Subscriptions: Carol McCauley & Brooklynn Hook; Advertising: Brooklynn Hook. For advertising rates, direct inquiries to info@pulpliterature.com.

Cover painting, *Dreaming Underwater* by Claire Lawrence. Artwork for 'Then and Now: An ASD Comic' by Matthew Nielsen. All other illustrations by Mel Anastasiou.

Pulp Literature: ISSN 2292-2164 (Print), ISSN 2292-2172 (Digital), Issue No. 39, Summer 2023.

Published quarterly by Pulp Literature Press, 21955 16 Ave, Langley, BC, Canada V2Z 1K5, pulpliterature.com, at $15.00 per copy. Annual subscription $50.00 in Canada, $72.00 in continental USA, $86.00 elsewhere. Printed in Victoria, BC, Canada, by First Choice Books / Victoria Bindery.

Pulp Literature Press gratefully acknowledges the support of the Canada Council for the Arts.

Pulp Literature is a proud member of the Magazine Association of BC and Magazines Canada.

TABLE OF CONTENTS

FROM THE PULP LIT PULPIT

Perchance to Write

Franz Kafka, in a letter to his fiancée, told her, "One can never be alone enough when one writes ... there can never be enough silence around one when one writes ... even night is not enough." I may be more of a morning person, but I get it. He meets her offer of company with much the same attitude as the sentiment on my coffee mug greets those who deign to enter my writer's cave: F*** off, I'm writing.

But even after wrangling the necessary solitude, the writer's battle is still only half-won. There's still the fact of basic biology to wrestle with. In a diary entry dated November 15, 1910, Kafka, ever the night owl, vowed, "I won't let myself get tired. I will jump into my novella even if it should cut up my face." Talk about dedication to the craft!

Writers can surely relate, or at least aspire, to this hunger, but many readers understand it too. The desire to remain in the magical web cast by a well-spun story. To better know a newfound literary companion. To stay lost in a faraway land as long as the clock and tiring eyes will allow. I think of the cartoon characters of my childhood, their eyes bloodshot and propped open by toothpicks. Cutting up the face, indeed.

Whether we rise with the robins or stay up late with the nightingales, the rhythm of darkness and light patterns our days and our seasons. And, let's be honest: our moods too. At least for now, summer is here and daylight lingers long. So, to the writers seeking inspiration for the next line and the readers ready to turn the next page, thank you for choosing to spend some of your time and precious solitude with us.

~Genevieve Wynand

In this issue

Swim away with story and let the enchantment begin with *Dreaming Underwater* by cover artist (and winner of the 2023 Magpie Award for Poetry!) **Claire Lawrence.**

Friendship carries us forward in 'The Drink We Spill Out on the Ground' by feature author **Claire Humphrey**, 'A Summer Soup to Cure Magical Thinking' by **Kim Harbridge**, and *Stella Ryman and the Curse of Youth* by **Mel Anastasiou.**

Meanwhile, 'Marty' by **Kevin Sandefur**, 'When a Man Knows Much More than We Ever Did' by **Kelli Allen**, and 'Mayflies' by **Liza Potvin** remind us that family life offers its own kind of adventures.

Jennifer Lott, with 'Thirty Minutes to Live', and **Beatrice Morgan**, with '6-Minute Quiz: What Percentage Monster are You?', show us how to make wise use of our time. **Matthew Nielsen**'s 'Then and Now: An ASD Comic' and **Soramimi Hanarejima**'s 'Vulnerability, Now and Then' offer up a spectrum of possibility. And, with 'The Golden Calf', **JM Landels** shows us another side of friendship and duty.

Poetry by **Elina Taillon**, **Haro Lee**, and **DS Martin** takes us to the moon and madness. Then 'Reap What You Sow' by **Alex Reece Abbott** and 'Tourist Trap at the End of the World' by **KT Wagner** land us back on (somewhat) solid ground.

Allaigna's Song
Overture
J M Landels

PULP
Literature
JJ Lee
'The Man in the Long Black Coat'

PULP
Literature
Carol Berg
'Uncanonical Murder'

PULP
Literature
Matthew Hughes
'The Devil You Don't'

Allaigna's Song: Aria

PULP
Literature
George McWhirter
'Stalk'

THE DRINK WE SPILL OUT ON THE GROUND

Claire Humphrey

***Claire Humphrey**'s first novel,* Spells of Blood and Kin, *won the 2017 Sunburst Award. Her short fiction has appeared in* Strange Horizons, Beneath Ceaseless Skies, Apex, Crossed Genres, Fantasy Magazine, *and* Podcastle. *Her short story 'Bleaker Collegiate Presents an All-Female Production of Waiting for Godot' appeared in the Lambda Award-nominated collection Beyond Binary, and her short story 'The Witch Of Tarup' was published in the critically acclaimed anthology* Long Hidden.

The Drink We Spill Out on the Ground

The perfect day looks like this: I wake up in the spare room at my boyfriend's family home. I tie my hair in a messy ponytail and stumble downstairs. Étienne plays his guitar by the window, sunlight filtering through the pine branches, a half cup of coffee on the sill. André sits on the counter, waiting for his toast, drumming his hands on the cupboard door. And I begin to hum along.

The perfect day is a snapshot beginning to crease, edges smudged with thumbprints. Me, Étienne, and André, together in the late morning, making music.

I remember thinking, the day I went down to the culvert, how lucky we were. Not even out of high school and already we had this.

I knew about change, a little. I knew I didn't want it.

I knew how to make a wish and make it stick.

Cherry brandy, crusty around the cap, only a quarter full: it was from the very back of Mrs Thibodeau's liquor cabinet. I tucked it in my music case when no one was looking, between a sheaf of loose scores and a practice book.

Once Étienne and André were busy with their PlayStation, I hopped the low wall at the back of their yard and handed myself down the slope, tree trunk to tree trunk.

Étienne showed me the way one afternoon while André was playing shinny. He led me down through tangles of wild grapevines and over mossy limestone blocks. We descended the crumbled face of what had once been an inclined wall, until my reaching foot met the arch of the culvert.

Étienne didn't know what it was for. He and André had made a fort there when they were kids. Now that they were no longer kids, they went down there to smoke joints when their mother was home.

The libation wasn't a thing to them. Étienne just didn't like the last swallow at the bottom of a can. That first day, we only had one: a Labatt's Genuine Draft he'd liberated from the guy who rented the Thibodeaus' carriage house. We passed it around until there was an inch left, warm and foamy, and then Étienne emptied it onto the broken floor of the culvert.

I was the one who had felt the chilly air breathing out from beneath the city's stones. I was the one who had studied the classics and knew how to get the attention of gods.

The brambles had grown thicker since my last visit. I could see where Étienne and André had kicked a pathway, but it stopped on the lip of the culvert in a scattering of cigarette butts. I paused for a moment to look down at the muscular curves of the river, and then I slithered down the bank.

Someone else had been here recently. The ashes of a makeshift campfire still smouldered. A sleeping bag had been rolled out on the rotted mattress at the edge of the light. An empty can lay beside the fire: alphabet noodles.

I couldn't see very far into the dimness of the culvert. The person who'd been sleeping here could be there, watching me from the dark.

I fumbled my bag open and found the bottle. The cherry brandy tasted like hangover breath. I spat it out on the stones.

I made my wish then. I held that perfect morning in my mind's eye and said *this, this, this. For all time.*

There was no answer. The slow breath of air from under the city didn't change.

Maybe I needed to give something more.

I pulled out my wallet. It contained a single twenty. More than I'd earn for a gig, more than I'd earn for an evening of babysitting. More than a bus ticket to visit my mom.

I rolled the bill into a cylinder and tucked it in one of the rusting coils of the mattress-spring.

Was the air from underground a little warmer? Was that a distant train, that low hollow wail?

My nerve broke, and I fled the culvert for the fresh air outside, scrambling back up the slope.

But up at the top of the rise was the Thibodeau house and my perfect day, waiting for me to step back in.

I knew Étienne before I knew André. Étienne was in his final year: a year older than me. He and his buddies held court at the same coffee shop where a bunch of us from the music wing spent our spares.

Étienne and I shared a love of rock from the seventies. We both took our coffee black. We both wore our hair long and straight.

Étienne was the one who taught me euchre. Étienne was the one who brought me into his band when he learned I could sing through my flute like Ian Anderson.

André was the one I fucked.

We had a different bass player every couple of months. Étienne did guitar and vocals, André played drums, I was on flute and backup, and most recently there was Konstantin, who was nineteen and shy and wore wire-rimmed glasses.

Konstantin told us about the gig while he was tuning up: said it, barely audible over his own bass, from behind the cloud of his curly dark hair.

"No shit," André said, dropping his sticks. "Seriously, a hundred bucks?"

"I know the going rate's more," Konstantin said, "but it's just a house party. My cousin, he's leaving town."

Étienne set his palm to André's shoulder to shut him up. "Maybe," he said. "As a favour to your cousin."

Konstantin ducked his head further down. "I can cancel, if it's not enough …"

"Nah," Étienne said. "We can swing it this once. If your cousin promises to get us drunk. April likes Johnnie Walker."

Konstantin rolled a dubious eye in my direction.

"Straight up," I said. I grinned at Konstantin. I always liked the bass players: they were strangers, which made me more like one of the group.

Étienne shook out a handful of coiled cable. "Half-hour set?" he said.

Konstantin nodded. "We've got a few weeks for me to get up to speed, right?"

"Should be fine," Étienne said. "Let's start with 'Thick as a Brick'. Ready, April?"

I settled the mouthpiece of my flute under my lower lip, and we swung into the song.

Étienne had the opening, a quick acoustic patter and a first line that showcased his beguiling voice.

I came in a moment later. The flute line, light and pretty, twined in with Étienne's, split apart for a delicious pause to let him shine, and then it was my turn again, dancing over the flickering guitar until Konstantin came in with a thumping bass chord.

André's part in this tune was almost nothing, a bit of brush, but he still managed to miss his entrance. I glared over at him to see he was just kind of glassily sitting there: smoked up before practice again, probably. He caught the movement of my head and winced an apology.

I turned my back on him and went back to watching Étienne.

We hadn't played a gig with Konstantin yet, so we put in some extra practice. One Saturday, Konstantin and I both showed up before Étienne and André were even awake.

Mrs Thibodeau let us in, yawning, and parked us in the kitchen nook. "I should give you your own mug at this rate," she said to Konstantin, rummaging in the cupboard for a plain dark blue one. "Here. Matches your eyes."

My own mug had a lamb sitting in a clump of daffodils—Mrs Thibodeau's idea of cute, because of my name.

"Have you got your university applications in yet?" she asked Konstantin.

I knew he'd done jack shit about it so far, but he smiled, ducking behind his hair a little. "Working on it, ma'am."

"It's quite a process, isn't it? Maybe you can give Étienne a friendly nudge."

"I thought he was staying here and going to Merritt College," I said.

"He can do better than that. My boys can do better," she said.

Konstantin gave me a startled look. So I wasn't the only one who noticed the edge to her tone.

She was all nice again a moment later, offering us the sugar, putting some waffles in the toaster for André when he slouched downstairs.

But when Étienne followed, knuckling at his temple, she said, loud and sweet, "How about a big plate of eggs, dear?" And she pulled the blinds up to let in the morning light.

"Oh, God, Mom," Étienne said, hands over his eyes, and she laughed and laughed, like it was the funniest hangover ever.

Konstantin's cousin Nick was the last tenant in the condemned house. Tomorrow, the demolition would start.

The landlord had long since stopped doing maintenance. The porch roof sagged, and the screen of the front door was ripped in a ragged X. Inside, the carpet had worn through to the subfloor.

The two main rooms were joined by a big open arch. No furniture—Nick's stuff was already moved out—but the gear was all set up for us to play later.

In the kitchen someone had lined up about a hundred 'Proud Canadian' stickers on the cupboards. Those stickers come free on bottles of rye. There wasn't any rye, though, just the shitty leftovers of people's liquor cabinets. Étienne, André, Konstantin, and Cousin Nick were already by the keg.

I went to André and hip-checked him and kissed his shoulder. When I looked up, I saw Cousin Nick's puzzled eyes go from me to André to Étienne. He muttered something to Konstantin, who laughed and said, "That's what I thought, too."

I turned away from all of them and filled my red plastic cup from the kitchen tap.

When I turned back, I saw Étienne with a bottle in each hand, filling his cup with clear ouzo and dark brown Kahlúa. I stuck my tongue out in disgust. He grinned, shook out the last few drops from the ouzo bottle, and tossed it out the open back door.

I heard it smash on the deck. I raised my eyebrows.

"This whole place will be wrecked tomorrow," Étienne reminded me.

"You'll be wrecked tomorrow," I said, as he tipped back a slug of his drink.

He flinched at the taste, shook it off with a shudder that went from scalp to spine. "Yeah!" He slung his arm around André's shoulders and stuck his tongue out for Konstantin's camera.

Showtime. Konstantin tuned his bass, André fidgeted with his hi-hat, and I edged around, placing the mics.

Étienne was still outside.

André had been out to call him and got a bottle smashed at his feet. My turn, then.

In the backyard, the air was heavy with sulphur from the paper mill, cut through with puke. Étienne leaned over the fence, head against his folded arms.

"Wow," I said. "Would it be mean to say I told you so?"

I came close and drew the hanging locks of his hair back over his shoulder so I could see his face. Eyes closed, mouth open.

"I can tell everyone you're sick."

He reeled upright, grabbing at the fence. "No. I'm going to fucking sing."

"Better lose that shirt, then."

He wiped his mouth on the hem, pulled the damp mess off, and tossed it on the ground. Turned to me with his lean chest bared, defiant grin sloping off his face. Threw his arms around me and lifted me right off the ground.

I hugged him back, ignoring the smell that hung around him, and said into his ear, "Don't ever change."

I never remember the on-stage part of gigs very well. I get into this focused state, and then suddenly I'm on the other side of it, flute dripping with spit and condensation, the crowd's applause already dying off.

What I remember about this gig, the condemned house party, is how it looked to see Étienne out ahead of me, mic cord wrapped around his arm and over one bare shoulder, all the little muscles over his ribs knotting up with the force of his voice. Sweat flying from the locks of his hair.

I remember André, too, a little. He played with his mouth open like a tragedy mask.

I don't remember what Konstantin looked like, but I sure remember how he sounded, the heavy energy of his final line.

I stood there buzzing as the reverb started to fade and the people in the house hooted and clapped. Étienne let the mic dangle from a loose hand.

Then he swung it up again and said, "You guys know this house is going to be demo'd."

Cheers from the crowd.

"You guys ever want to fuck shit up?"

More cheers. I had my flute hugged close across my chest.

"Do it!" called Cousin Nick, grinning. "Do it!"

"Fucking right!" Étienne shouted. "Let's do it."

The last of his words went quiet as Étienne stepped on the mic cord and ripped it from the amp, but it didn't matter: the people in front of me exploded like shrapnel, tearing into the walls of the house with their fists and boots and bottles.

I turned to blink at André, but he had his eyes on his brother like everyone else. He jumped up from behind his kit, picked up his stool, and whirled it into the wall.

I woke up in the wrecked house with my head on André's boot.

I sat up. Someone else's baseball hat fell off my head. I shook André's foot, and he mumbled and drew his arm over his eyes. His face was grey-white with drywall dust on one side.

Konstantin was curled right next to us, one arm thrown across André's stomach. I rummaged in Konstantin's discarded army-surplus jacket until I found his camera, and I shot them both like that: shirts twisted around their bodies, splinters caught in their hair.

Other people were sleeping all over the place. I stepped over splayed legs and crooked arms, taking pictures.

Our gear was okay, shoved in the corner and barricaded by a door torn off its hinges. The door had a poster of Jim Morrison on it; both of his eyes had been scraped out, and someone had drawn a giant doob in his mouth. I looked behind it, but Étienne wasn't back there.

In the kitchen, the keg stood majestic, the only upright thing amid a litter of toppled bottles and crushed cups. I tried to drink from the tap, but the water had been turned off.

Étienne wasn't out in the yard, either. The patio stones were almost invisible under drifts of broken glass, brown and clear and a salting of green all mingled like beach sand.

I walked out through the shattered maw where the front door had been.

Étienne wasn't on the front porch of his house, and the door was locked. But I found him in the back garden, sprawled on a chaise despite the chill, a white napkin wrapped around his wrist.

"What happened?" I said.

He shrugged. "Hope my tetanus shot is up to date."

"I woke up and you weren't there, and I was worried."

He lit a cigarette for me and another for himself. Shook his head, tangled hair sliding around his shoulders.

"A weird thing," he said. "I'll tell you about it if you promise you won't laugh."

"Of course," I said, sitting on the cold grass beside him, almost close enough to touch.

"Yeah … So. I woke up in the bathtub this morning, still fucked up. I wanted to go home. But I didn't have my key or my wallet or anything, and Mom's away, so I couldn't get in. I went down to the culvert, thought maybe it'd be warmer in there. And I tripped on this goddamn mattress and slashed my arm open." He gestured at his bandaged wrist. "So I'm lying there on this homeless guy's gross bed, bleeding, hung over as shit, and I knew, totally knew, this town would kill me if I stayed. And I wished I had a clue what to do."

"Did you … get a clue?"

"That was the weird part," he said, smoke breathing out with the words. "I was just, like, swearing, and slamming my hand on the ground. And twenty bucks fell out from somewhere, like magic. So I went to get a coffee."

"And the coffee told you what to do?" I said, trying to grin.

"Mike Bainbridge did," he said. "He was at the coffee shop. Back for the weekend to see his folks. It turns out the degree program he's in is really awesome, so I'm going to apply."

"Simple as that," I said.

"Simple as that," he echoed, and ground out his cigarette in the ornamental kale.

I went down to the culvert again to see if I could fix it. I couldn't even feel the chill from underground now, though. The ashes of the campfire were scattered, the empty tins had rusted, and the curtain of wild grapes that hid the entrance had withered and shrunk away, letting in pale sunlight.

I could see the stains on the ground where I'd spilled the libation. I wetted them again, made the same wish, just to be sure. Nothing happened.

Later I thought about spilling blood, myself. I figured if anything could break the wish or the bond or whatever, and make a new one, that must be it.

But then Étienne got a crested envelope containing his university acceptance, and I saw his face when he opened it.

André and Konstantin and I still get together to practise, but we mostly just jam and talk shit and smoke up. We haven't played a single gig since Étienne left.

Étienne says he'll be back for Thanksgiving, but we know he won't be: it will be this other version of him, with shorter hair and a pile of textbooks. He'll be bringing some friends from school with him. One of them's a girl.

With him gone, you might think André and I would get closer, but it's pretty much the same as always. We get together, we sleep together, it's fine. He's a good guy.

But I'm afraid one day I'm going to trip on something that will tear me open, and change will enter my bloodstream like rust and eat away what's keeping me here. Or maybe it will happen to André first.

I'm not sure which would be worse. Watching him leave — or watching him stay, in his basement jam room with his bong, while upstairs his mom gets more gray hair, and Étienne comes home less, and I send messages from some other city where I have a new boyfriend who doesn't have a brother.

What's the word for it again, when something you know starts to look unfamiliar?

FEATURE INTERVIEW

Claire Humphrey

Pulp Literature: *This story feels to me like it took place in the 1990s, though perhaps I am projecting—and revealing my age! The people are recognizable, the friendships relatable. What was the inspiration for this story? Did you have to change any names to protect the innocent and unwitting?*

Claire Humphrey: You're entirely correct. A few of the elements of this story were drawn directly from my own high school experience in the early 90s. I was, briefly, the flute player in a Jethro Tull cover band, although we didn't actually ever play a gig as far as I recall, and what I mostly remember is learning the music alone at home by playing along with a pirated cassette. And I did attend a party in a condemned apartment which devolved into wrecking the place. The characters in the story share some superficial elements with people I knew, but there are no direct representations.

The house overhanging the ravine is a real place. I almost always write about real places. The culvert is also real. There's a true and much sadder story about a twenty-dollar bill that no one would believe if I shared it, and it haunts me still. The true story only appears here as a transmuted symbol and a feeling, one I think a lot of my friends of that time would recognize: the feeling that some of us were not getting out of that town alive. Unlike the protagonist, I did. But it was a tough place to grow up, with a lot of substance abuse, bigotry, and economic depression, and not everyone was able to thrive or even survive.

PL: *What are your rules for writing about other people?*

CH: I never do, and I always do. My mother used to ask me whether she was the mother in my stories, especially when there was a mother doing something unpleasant, which worried her. She was never the mother in the story. She never thought to ask whether she was the house, or the wizard, or the goose.

Even when I write about an event someone else in my life might recognize in some way, I hope they realize that by the time the superficially factual has passed through my fiction mill, none of it is about them anymore. Only, of course, anyone who has touched my life is in here somewhere.

PL: *How long does it typically take you to write a short story? How long to edit it? Are these discrete stages of the writing process for you, or do you revise as you go?*

CH: It varies by story. I've written a few hard-burn drafts from start to finish in a day or two, which have ended up published with very few edits. I've also written incredibly laborious stories with a dozen rounds of revisions. I usually get critiques from other writers, which are very helpful. This story was submitted to another magazine in an earlier draft, and I was lucky to get a good critique from an editor who didn't buy it, but whose advice made it stronger. Although I'm not a new writer anymore, I still don't always know my own story's needs, and sometimes rush things to submission or get stuck in fruitless revisions before finding the right set of eyes to help me get the story right.

PL: *On a 'good' day, how much can you write?*

CH: On a good day, a thousand words. On a great day, I've topped out at almost ten thousand—but that's when I've bought myself uninterruptible time at a retreat, where I can start my day with a workout and a huge breakfast, and finish it with an ocean view and a microbrew. Those days are treasures. And I have to admit there are lots of days when I don't write at all.

PL: *On the harder days, have you ever thought about giving it up? What gets you back to the page?*

CH: I honestly don't have much trouble writing, when I'm writing. The hard days for me are when I realize there's been a stretch of time without it: not because I didn't want to write, or couldn't, but because I failed to carve out the time from my job, my family and friends, my self-care, my volunteer demands. I question my own choices often, but writing draws me back because I love it more than anything else.

PL: *As a writer of both novels and short stories, do you find that there are any similarities or differences between how you approach the blank page for each?*

CH: I used to approach them the same way: by starting out with a strong first sentence and asking myself who said it, or who it's about, and then feeling my way through how long that person's story needed to be. Now I outline when I'm writing longer work, because

I can be so much more efficient that way. I don't do a very detailed outline, but I give myself some big beats and set some intentions for what happens in between them. With short stories, I still feel my way through and let myself have more fun with the structure.

PL: *Who are your trusted first readers?*

CH: I have a very dear friend who gets to read everything before anyone else; she's first because she deeply understands and loves what I do. Her blessing means a lot. Once I know she loves a story, I'm ready to seek a tougher reception from the next few readers. I recently started working with a new in-person group, and I'm delighted to be doing that again. I also belong to an online group where we can share critiques ad hoc.

PL: *Are there any stories living inside of you, nagging to be told?*

CH: Always! I hope that well never runs dry. But I think you're asking more specifically about stories that are close to the surface but not yet fully broken through, right? The one that stands out right now is a novel I began several years ago, where I rewrote the first few chapters several times with totally different approaches, and never quite figured out how to proceed. I reread it sometimes and am still hoping it will settle into something I can continue, but it's a big challenge: it's set in an alternate-world, early-twentieth-century North America where the USA is basically a Puritan country and Canada is primarily Quaker, and they're at war with each other. There are a few huge problems with this idea, and with me being the one to write it. The biggest one is that I am a lifelong atheist and really don't have a deep understanding of how religious people feel, which means I'm probably not doing these characters justice. I doubt I will finish this book unless something about the characters and setting changes materially—and if that happens, will it still be this book?

PL: *Thank you for making the time to speak with us. Before we go, tell us, what are you working on now?*

CH: A dark fantasy novel that combines Celtic mythology with the challenges of a blended family running a small business and dealing with old crimes that won't stay buried. Also, a short story about a robot who smokes cigarettes.

Select Bibliography

Spells of Blood and Kin, Macmillan, 2016
'The State Street Robot Factory', *Apex,* 2023
'We Are the Flower', *Podcastle,* 2020
'Our Cousins, Whom We Do Not Use as Directed', *Flash Fiction Online,* 2019
'Number One Draft Pick', *The Sum of Us,* 2017
'Le lundi de la matraque (Nightstick Monday)', *Strange Horizons,* 2017
'Dinners in Wartime', *Liminal Stories,* 2017
'Yellowcat', *Grain Magazine,* 2017
'Wooden Boxes Lined with the Tongues of Doves', *Beneath Ceaseless Skies,* 2017

For a complete list of works, visit clairehumphrey.ca/writing/

RESTRAINING ORDER AGAINST THE MOON

Elina Taillon

Elina Taillon *is a queer, neurodiverse MFA candidate in UBC's Creative Writing program and former managing editor at* PRISM international. *Elina holds a master's degree in French literature from the University of Toronto. Elina's prose is published in* Déraciné *and* filling Station, *and her poetry appears in* CV2, The /tɛmz/ Review, *and* Grain.

Restraining order against the moon

because I saw you peering
a tunnel through the tree branches
yellow-eyed staring
winking behind another building

and because I noticed you while sprawled
on the couch next to my charging
phone and laptop, corn chip dust
under my fingernails, and because

you have no business spying
now, or the time I ate macaroni
out of a wine glass, or when
I cut my hair laughing, tearstained,
took fifteen minutes to open a can,
flicked a fingernail clipping
towards a pile and missed
and didn't pick it up off the floor,
held a previous tenant's mail
against a flashlight to read

their personal information,
moved naked through your light,
spied on you from beneath my sheets,

because now there's a heap of plates
covered in cheese grease in the sink
and all you can do is
shred yourself behind my blinds
(I am your lost custody battle),
purse your lips
aim at my cluttered windowsill
blow the shrivelling holly berries
into the sink with a plunk and plop,

I will stare back.
I'll remember you in your hues
of white and blue and red and beige,
note down times and dates,
your garb of clouds and smog.
and in the morning,
I'll tell the sun.

THE GOLDEN CALF

JM Landels

***JM Landels** is the author of the bestselling Allaigna's Song trilogy, and her spy novel,* The Shepherdess, *is currently serialized in even-numbered issues of this magazine. 'The Golden Calf' is a crossover of sorts between the two. Set in Allaigna's world of the Ilmar, it recounts a little-known history of her stepfather, Duke Allenis Andreg, and it is also about a herder—though of cattle, not sheep. JM herself stays away from ruminants but does keep a small herd of horses at her farm in Langley, BC, where she teaches mounted combat and wages an ongoing war against buttercups. You can find @jmlandels on most social media platforms, or at jmlandels.stiffbunnies.com.*

The Golden Calf

Saoira hoists the morning's last two buckets with her yoke and carries them into the cool shade of the stone-walled creamery. It's early in the day, but already the Garelan sun is making the air uncomfortably warm, even up here in the Rillonna highlands. She'd best hurry and get the ladies moving before it's too hot to walk. With the morning's milk capped and settling next to the ice room, she takes up her stick and pack, whistles to Isa, and the two of them begin to herd the half dozen cows and their calves up to the high pasture for the day.

It's only an hour's walk, but by the time they make it to the meadow, even the calves have stopped gambolling and are ready to rest in the shade of the whispering aspens while their mothers enthusiastically crop the sweet high-meadow grass.

Saoira sets down her pack in the tiny hut near the tree line, before she heads out behind it with a white-enamelled cup in hand. She scoops a cup of water from a snow-fed rillet that trickles between the trees on its way to the valley. Settling on the smooth grey stone overlooking the meadow, she sips icy water. The amenities here are even more primitive than at the creamery below, but she wishes she could stay here all summer, day and night, without the daily trek. She'd let the cows' milk decrease so they only had to feed their calves, and all of them would have a life of ease.

But then winter would come, as it always does, and hay would need to be bought, and the milk would dry up as the calves weaned themselves, and she would need to pay farmers Ellick or Roent for their bulls to cover her cows ... and all that takes money that her mother brings in by selling cheese and butter at the market. So Saoira will herd the cattle back down to the dairy tonight, where they can be milked again and shut in their pens till morning. And Saoira will sleep in her straw bed in the safety of a house.

Just as her thoughts come to this inevitable and unsatisfying conclusion, they are interrupted by a sound that has no place here: another human voice—a man's—shouting in surprise, or perhaps anger, followed by the equally rare sound of galloping hooves that are far heavier and faster than any cow's. Seconds later, an enormous horse thunders over the rise and into the meadow, scattering the cows and sending the calves bucking off into the trees. The creature, shining like a polished copper kettle in the morning sun, zigs around lumbering cows straight towards Saoira.

She is on her feet, arms outstretched to make herself large and visible. The horse sees her, slides on its hocks, then zags to the left and begins to trot the perimeter of the meadow, nostrils wide, neck arched, and tail flowing like a flag, with the stirrups of the empty saddle bouncing in time. Furious at the beast, she ignores its high-strung display and marches across the meadow to the trailhead to see where the rider might be.

A string of curses reaches her ears before he comes into view. The dark curls of his hatless head appear first, followed by the enraged face of a young nobleman. Noble, not just by the gold earrings, starched white collar—now mashed on one side—and dirtied but very rich clothes, but by the accent with which he delivers his curses.

To his credit, the swearing stops mid-phrase as he catches sight of Saoira. He reaches for his hat, realizes he's lost it, but sweeps a courtly bow nonetheless.

"A thousand apologies, mistress," he says in a voice as smooth and rich as it was harsh and vulgar a moment ago. "I seem to have mislaid my horse."

With impeccable timing, the creature in question trots past them in its spirited tour of the pasture. Neither human attempts to stop it. The stallion, for that is clearly what it is, will tire and graze soon enough.

"That horse?" Saoira asks, caught between amusement and annoyance but leaning to the latter for the upset it's caused her herd.

Isa, loyal hound that she is, hasn't moved from her mistress's side, though her darting eye shows she longs to bring that copper menace under control, and a low rankle in her throat expresses her suspicion of the man in front of her.

Saoira puts her hands on her hips. "It's frightened my cattle and scattered them into the wood. Isa and I will have to spend the rest of the day looking for them." That's not quite true. She can hear Maireg's bell not too far away, and if she can hear it, so can the rest of the cows. Isa will bring Maireg back easily, and the rest will find Maireg. But first she wants an apology from this fine young man who's landed his arse near her meadow.

He clears his throat. "All my apologies, mistress. I will gladly help you seek out your cattle, and reimburse you for any that are lost."

She raises an eyebrow, wondering if she can keep a few from returning to Maireg's bell straight away.

"I'll take that help, sir," she says. "But first we'd best catch your horse."

The chestnut stallion tires himself out and begins to crop the sweet meadow grass, but not before stepping on his rein and breaking it. Though Saoira knows next to nothing about horses, it's clear the beast is as green as the forage he's eating and will be no use rounding up cattle. She lends the young lord a rope from the collection of items she keeps in her hut, so that he may tether the animal to a tree. She watches awhile as he fumbles with knots before she takes the rope back.

"No," she says. "The knot around his neck needs to go under, around, and down—like this—so it won't slip and choke him." She tugs on the rope to demonstrate. "And this end," she says, tossing the rope over a branch and around the trunk so it can't slide down, "needs to be a knot you can undo with one hand."

All the while she's tying the rope, the horse fidgets, pulling away then shoving her with his head. At last she swats the animal's nose, and it jerks away. The rope around the tree tightens, but the one around the horse's neck does not, and neither come undone.

"See?" She puts on an outward air of authority but is quaking inside. The stallion seems as strong as a bull and far less sensible. She hopes he doesn't pull out the tree by its roots.

But the horse seems to have been trained to tie, or at least senses the struggle is not worth the effort, and stretches his long face down to the tall grass growing at the base of the tree. He can just reach it with his nimble lips.

"Let's get my cattle back, and then I'll help you fix that rein," she says, dusting her hands on her breeches, wondering that she has the temerity to order around someone so far above her station.

When Saoira and the lord emerge from the trees with the last wayward calf, they are both sweating, though him the more under his heavy clothing. Still, she is surprised by how fit he is for someone who must have a life of considerable ease.

She checks her cattle for injuries and finds none but a superficial scrape on the hock of the last bullock. Her shoulders relax at last.

"Is it serious?" the man asks, startling her. He is standing over her, peering down in consternation.

She stands, smiling to put him at ease. "It should heal fine. He just might not win any prizes in the show ring." Which is true enough, since this fellow will be sold for meat before he starts consuming her winter supply of hay.

The young lord apologizes for what must be the tenth time this morning, and she's sorry the wish for an apology ever crossed her mind. She waves it off and invites him to sit by the hut while she rummages through her collection of odds and ends for a scrap of leather and a lace with which to mend the horse's broken rein.

"I'm embarrassed," he announces as she settles down beside him, awl and leather in one hand and a cup of spring water in the other. "I have no coin on my person with which to compensate you for your time and the injury to your bullock."

She takes a long drink from the cup and passes it to him while she searches for a reply. It is true that the girls will probably give less milk tonight, having had a scare and run off some of their morning grass. But it is a small price, in the end, for what has been a morning's diversion. In truth, all she would have done whilst watching the cattle is write more ill-formed poetry or reread her well-fingered copy of *The Eagle's Lament*, the only book she owns. Deciding on honesty, she tells him so as she punches holes in the leather with her awl.

While she works the lace through the holes, the lord gets up and moves his horse to another tree. She watches with half an eye and notes that he does a fair job with the knot this time, though the rope is now long enough for the horse to get his leg over it. Not her problem, should that happen, she determines. The lord returns with his waterskin and sits beside her once more.

She ties off the lace and tugs on the rein to test her work. "That should hold till you can take it to your saddler," she announces, handing the bridle back to him.

He takes it with a smile that brightens the shadowed space between his dark moustache and tight-curled beard. "The finest tailor in Aleran could make no stitches more pleasing to me. I'll keep this rein as it is, as a reminder of the fairest cowherd in the land."

She laughs, nervous for the first time today. Is he teasing her?

He's holding out the chipped enamel cup, which he has refilled from his skin. It is wine, not water, as deep red as afterbirth. She drinks wine twice a year: at the autumn market feast, and after the spring castration, when all the herders of Rillonna gather. And none of it is ever as sweet, rich, and peppery as this. She takes a second sip, and remembers her manners once more.

"Thank you, good sir."

"My name's Allenis," he says. "I don't know yours."

"Saoira," she replies.

"Just Sarah? What is your father's name?"

"Just Allenis?" she counters. "My father is dead or gone. I'm not sure which. I'm the daughter of Sorinna Little, who owns the creamery at the foot of the path you rode up and the dairy in Little Water."

He makes as deep a bow as he can from his seat on the stone. "Allenis Andreg, of Osthegn." He searches her face as if looking for some sign of recognition.

"In Teillai?" she asks. "You're a long way from home."

"I'm on a diplomatic envoy to Rillonna, and no doubt my friends at the Duchess's keep will be wondering why I missed breakfast and now lunch."

"Why did you?"

"I have some important decisions ahead. I needed to clear my head."

"On that beast? Couldn't you clear your head on something saner?"

"Talon is green, and fiery, but he only unseated me because my mind was far away when a rabbit dashed across our path."

She shrugs. "If you say so."

He laughs and stands. "I would I could stay here all day, Lady Saoira Little, but I have missed two meals with my host and dare not miss a third."

"In that case"—she stands as well and brushes off her breeches—"you'd best take some cheese with you."

She goes into her hut and emerges with a small, cloth-wrapped square. She opens the wrapping to reveal the soft black rind. "Little Water Ash," she says. "It's hard to find, even in Little Water. But I always keep a few back from the market."

He takes it with a puzzled air and brings it to his nose.

"Try it." She reaches over and breaks off a corner to reveal the creamy beige inside.

"Cinders and all?" he asks as he takes the morsel from her.

"Cinders and all."

His smile expands as he savours the soft cheese. "I am indebted to you all over again, Lady Saoira. I will see the Duchess of Rillonna stocks her boards with Little Water Ash."

"If she can get it." She shrugs and laughs.

Two days later, with the heavy, itchy feeling of a much-needed thunderstorm weighing the air, the copper-coloured stallion appears at the crest of the trail, this time carrying his rider.

Saoira, sitting on her rock stoop, a board with a much-rescraped piece of parchment on her lap, is working on a poem. It is slow writing with a thin duck-feather as a quill and lumpy ink made from thimbleberries. But the ink, though uneven and impermanent on the worn parchment, is a pleasant violet, and her words, for once, please her.

Isa's bark alerts her to the horse and rider, and spooks the former. At least the latter keeps his seat as his horse scoots sideways and then prances diagonally through the meadow. This time, the cows barely look up.

"Isa, heel!" Saoira calls, hurriedly capping her ink pot and tucking the evidence of her poesy inside the hut.

As the horse dances its way towards her, she considers whether she should curtsy now that she knows the identity of the young man. She decides against it. She's not in the habit of courtly gestures, and she sees no reason to set a precedent now. So she waits, Isa at her side, doing her best to imitate a cow's soft and placid expression as she watches her visitor approach.

Allenis has recovered his hat, or acquired a new one. In fact, his clothing is even finer than last time, and not just because it has not made recent contact with the ground. He sweeps the magnificent plumed hat from his head and bows from the saddle before vaulting to the ground and repeating the bow.

"Mistress Saoira," he says, "I'm glad to find you here again."

"I'm here all summer, Lord Allenis, weather permitting." She glances at the thunderheads building in the west but is suddenly glad she drove the cows up this morning despite the ominous clouds.

"Well, I stopped at the creamery first."

She raised an eyebrow, unsure of how she feels about a nobleman visiting her home in her absence.

"I have left a token of thanks for you there. But I thought it better to tell you in person rather than leave a note."

"In case I can't read, you mean?"

His light brown cheeks darken in embarrassment. "I would never assume …" For the first time, his words stumble.

She decides to rescue him, smiling to let him know she's not offended. "Not many cowherds can read, I admit. But I can."

"And write as well, I see." He importunately takes hold of her right hand and examines her ink-stained fingers. "These are the fingers of a scribe, not a cowherd." He brings them to his lips and kisses them with a mere whisper of breath. "But they smell sweeter than either."

She stares at him a moment, lost for words for once in her life, before taking her hand back. She brings her fingers to her own lips. They smell of sweet milk, grass, and berries. She realizes she is blushing.

He saves her from speaking. "I ride for Teillai tomorrow, but I will return in a few moons. Might I order some Little Water Ash to take back for the midwinter feast?"

"How much?" she asks, surprised out of her sudden shyness.

He has thought this through, for he answers immediately. "Five dozen like the one you gave me ought to do."

It is a huge amount of cheese. Her mother makes around a hundred and fifty of that Ash each season, for it doesn't keep or travel well. She tells him as much.

"The temperature at midwinter should keep it fresh, and I will be travelling by fast coach."

She then explains how the cows give hardly any milk in the winter; and she will have to store his boxes of cheese in the ice house, long past the time she would have sold them at the autumn markets; and they will ripen, even in the cold, and change their flavour.

"It is a large risk, I know," he interrupts, "setting aside a third of your output for a client who may or may not show up, and may not get the cheese he remembers."

He reaches into the purse at his belt. "I'm willing to take a gamble on the condition of the cheese if you're willing to gamble on me as a buyer. You were right: I couldn't find a single Little Water Ash at any of the cheesemongers in Rillonna. But they told me what it sells for." He takes her hand and places three gold eagles in the palm. "This should cover your production costs. And I will pay you the difference between that and the full market price, directly, when I collect them in Ceron."

She should protest. Cheesemaking is a fickle task. Weather, both long and short term, affects the cows' diets, the behaviour of the cultures her mother uses, how the cheeses set, and how they store. The fall cheeses will only taste similar, not identical, to the spring ones. But his face is so earnest, so happy, that she nods and promises him sixty cheeses.

As she pockets the three coins, fat drops of warm summer rain spatter her bare arms and the dry ground at their feet. Forgetting her manners, she swears at the roiling black clouds that have overtopped the mountain. There is a flicker of lightning and a not-long-enough wait for the inevitable rumble of thunder.

"I've got to get the girls back down the mountain," she says as she heads into the hut for her pack.

She could weather the storm here in the hut, but she'd rather get her cattle out of the exposed meadow. She sends Isa to rouse them. Saoira should have noticed them lying down in readiness for the weather, but she was too distracted by the handsome lord and his gold. She grabs her crook and shoulders her pack, dashing back out of the hut to shoo Tulip, the laziest of cows, who is still resting on her red-and-white belly, contentedly chewing her cud.

Allenis has mounted his horse, who is spinning in anxious circles as the cattle move past him.

"Get down!" she yells at him as another flash of lightning stutters across the sky. "You're too tall on that beast."

The rumble of thunder drowns anything either of them might say next, but he complies.

Isa has already got the cows moving down the trail, Maireg in the lead. Saoira slaps Tulip on the hindquarters with her staff, sending the cow into a lumbering trot to catch up. Saoira whoops, and the whole herd starts trotting. She waves at Allenis to follow, and he leads his horse after her.

The rain is coming faster now, pelting her head with fat warm drops and filling the air with the smell of hot earth and grass. She trots after her herd, skidding down the steep trail till they reach the Forks: two giant rocks—or rather one rock long ago split in two—that flank the path. Saoira whistles a halt, and

Isa, dashing between the legs of cows, heads to the front of the queue and stops Maireg. The other cows jumble around her but don't try to pass their leader. With the herd collected between the Forks, along with Allenis and his wild-eyed stallion, Saoira can breathe at last.

"We can wait out the storm here," she yells over the drumming of rain on rock. "Don't touch the stones," she warns as he places a hand against one rock to free a much smaller one from his boot. "The water running down can bring lightning."

He nods understanding, pulls his horse closer to the middle, and leans on his saddle to finish dealing with his boot. That done, he unties the bundle from the back of his saddle and unrolls a voluminous cloak. He tosses one edge over the saddle and holds the other side up with his arm, creating a tent between him and the horse.

"Join me?" he asks, motioning her in with his other arm.

She's already soaked through, and it's not cold, but she accepts his offer so as not to seem rude. She is nervous of the stallion, who snorts and tosses his head with each thunderclap but at least keeps his giant iron-shod feet still.

The smell of wet horse fills the space under Allenis's cloak. It is sweeter and more flowery than the slightly boozy smell of cows. And there is the smell of Allenis too: strange and no doubt expensive perfumes in his beard and clothes, but beneath those, the earthy smell of sweat. Not unpleasant, just very male and foreign to Saoira, who spends half her year alone and the rest with her mother.

When the clouds roll away as fast as they had come in, and the wet rocks glisten in sunlight, Saoira thanks Allenis and ducks out of the makeshift shelter, glad to breathe newly washed air and clear her head. As they waited under his cloak, his arm tired and he switched hands more than once. Each time she offered to take a turn holding it, and he gallantly refused, despite the fact they are of a height. The smell of his sweat and the steamy hide of the horse was pleasant and cloying at the same time. The fresh mountain air is far less confusing.

He shakes his cloak out and spreads it over his horse's back to dry.

"Would you like help herding them back up?" he asks.

Saoira casts an eye eastward. "There's more rain coming, and I'm a third of the way back down. They can have hay in the byre early today. And I need to see how much of the morning's milk has curdled."

"Then I shall walk with you, if I may." The sweep of his hat as he bows casts into the air drops of water that sparkle like diamonds.

They are all dry and the air is hot again by the time they reach the creamery. Saoira can feel the second storm in the offing already. As they approach the paddock gate, Isa sets off into the hay shed, barking.

Saoira swears she can hear the plaintive sound of a lost calf coming from the shed, but all six of hers are accounted for. She shuts the gate after her herd and hurries into the shed.

Standing there, knee deep in a pile of stored hay, is the most delicate calf she has ever seen. It gazes at her with enormous brown eyes and lets out another bawl, answered this time by one of Saoira's cows. She opens the door wide and shoos the calf out of her hay shed, cursing the idiot that shut a strange animal up on her property.

And then she remembers Allenis's words from this morning, before the storm and the trek back down—words that seem to have been spoken on another day altogether: "I left a token of thanks for you."

A token? She eyes the calf—not even a bullock, but an uncastrated bull calf—with growing apprehension. It is smaller than her own calves, but that is likely because of its breed, not its age. It seems to be the thin-skinned type that the Tiffin family south of Rillonna raise. A five-month old calf is not a token. The tawny cattle of the Tiffins fetch the highest price for breeding stock in all of Aerach. It is a gift too rich. And a liability. It would be criminal to castrate this fine animal and slaughter him for beef as she does her other male calves. But his pasterns and his coat are too thin for the rough mountain trails and harsh weather her herd withstands. Dare she sell a gift from a lord at the autumn market? And if she doesn't sell it, and doesn't slaughter it, she will have to feed it all winter alongside her cows, and then next summer keep him separate, for he'll want to cover them after their spring calves are born.

A heifer would still have been too rich a gift, but so much more welcome.

Saoira looks from the calf, who is being inspected by her girls, to Allenis, who is beaming at her and the burden he's inflicted upon her, and all she can do is smile and thank him.

The down payment of three gold eagles and the gift of the calf go only a little way to softening her mother's ire. She eyes her daughter up and down.

"You didn't tumble him, did you?"

"What business of yours would it be if I did?"

"He's left you with a wee bull to care for. You'd best see he doesn't leave you with a babe as well."

"Is that what my father did?" Saoira shoots back.

Her mother eyes her levelly. "Don't waste your whistle calling for cows that won't come. Nor get ideas above your station, neither." Saoira knows pursuing questions about her father is a dead end. Always has been, especially when her mother slips into her rural accent.

"Three gold eagles and a golden Tiffin calf seems a high price for some cheese he may not see," Saoira's mother observes, her voice returning to the educated clip of the merchant class. "You'd best take some of that coin and see if you can secure extra milk from our neighbours over the next few months. We may need another vat, and some new baskets as well if we're to supply your fancy man along with our regular customers. And I'll need your help in the evenings, unless we hire a new girl …"

They don't hire a new girl, and Saoira works twice as hard that autumn, tending the cattle, pressing apples, and helping her mother make cheese. In addition to a new vat, baskets, and an extra press, they increase the size of the cold room to add new shelves. This undertaking requires help from neighbouring farmers and villagers, who in turn require payment in cheese, butter, and cider. For, as her mother explains, they can't simply short their usual loyal customers, who deserve butter and cheese just as much as any lord. If the Littles don't supply it, people will go elsewhere, and next year, when fickle fine lords don't pay ahead for cheese, there will be no one to take it off their hands.

Saoira listens to this repeating litany in silence, her own stomach eating itself in worry as the eagles are used up and she and her mother dip into the supply of emergency silver. She eyes the bull calf who grows fatter on her winter hay, and not a day goes past she doesn't contemplate selling it. But it is the wrong time of year. Nobody wants another mouth to feed over winter, no matter the prizes the beast might win at the spring fair.

So she holds onto the bull calf and her worries, while the trees shed their leaves, the cold wind whips down from the peaks, and the ground turns white with snow.

What her mother doesn't know is that Allenis has been writing letters, and Saoira has been writing back. The first one was formal and courteous, thanking her yet again for her assistance in the mountains and assuring her of his return in the winter to collect the cheeses. Hers was equally formal, if less erudite, thanking him for his kind patronage and gift, and wishing him well.

His next one carried reminiscence of the warm summer day they met. She replied, smiling, with the memory of the thunderstorm on their second meeting, and thinks of how he stood close in the steamy air of the storm, smelling rich, exotic, and animal. And how he kissed her fingers before he left. She's no expert in hand kisses, having never experienced them before meeting him. But that last one rested soft lips and curly moustache against her knuckles for a full inhale and exhale, and left her feeling strange and unsheltered in her own barnyard.

Perhaps that memory made her letter seem more intimate than she intended, for his next contained details of his day-to-day life in Teillai, and soon after that, his day-to-day thoughts. It's not long before he's corresponding as if with an old friend.

When he arrives to pick up his order of cheese early in Ceron, he invites her to the Duchess's winter palace in Rillonna.

Wearing her only good dress and borrowed slippers, Saoira sits with Allenis in a sumptuous room filled with out-of-season flowers and eats a meal finer than any she has ever tasted, and which Allenis calls a light repast. She learns he is in Rillonna to court the Duchess's daughter for a betrothal which neither party wants, despite their parents' wishes. The Duchess's daughter is happy to entertain him, however, as his attentions distract her mother. And Allenis plays along, since the charade also keeps his father, the Duke of Teillai, happy. Allenis pays more than handsomely for his order of cheese and places a new order for the spring, when he will next be in Rillonna.

How can she say no?

Three times a year, Allenis visits Rillonna. Three times a year he meets with Saoira, and in the months in between, letters fly back and forth. The Littles' dairy expands, and Saoira and her mother work harder than ever.

Buttercup, as she's named the calf, grows to a bull and is even more trouble than he was as a calf. And still Saoira does not sell, castrate, or butcher him, because Allenis asks after him each time they meet. The first spring, Buttercup managed to break down three fence boards and cover two of her cows before she could separate them. One caught, and the result was a strange beast, with golden patches from her sire instead of the red-and-white coat from her dam. Still, three years down the road, when she is part of Saoira's herd, the milk she gives is richer than the rest, making Saoira wish, not for the first or last time, that Allenis had gifted her not a bull but a full-blooded Tiffin heifer.

After his adventure in her cows' paddock, Saoira leases Buttercup to her neighbours, who keep a small herd of bulls. In exchange for his upkeep, they sell his services and pass a third of the fee back to her. Buttercup is still hers, and she visits him a few times every fortnight with an apple or a heel of bread in her apron pocket. In this manner, they are happy to see one another, and she can report truthfully on his well-being to Allenis.

By the time her mother dies, Saoira and Allenis have become close enough friends that his is the shoulder she turns to in her grief. Generous as always, he offers financial support, which she turns down. Her mother set aside a portion of profits every year—often a tenth, sometimes only a twentieth, but since the dairy's expansion, usually more—to ensure Saoira would not need to sell, or marry to keep, the Little holdings. Reeth, the apprentice they took on two years back, is more than capable of running the dairy in Little Water so that Saoira can continue to tend her cattle. Buttercup's stud fees provide an extra cushion that Saoira sets aside in her mother's manner.

It is not gold she needs from Allenis, but solace. Reeth is pleasant enough company when the conversation turns around cattle and cream, milking and market days. But Allenis also lost his mother too young, despite all the doctors and tree-priests his father's deep pockets procured. In this way, as well as many others that have grown over the years, they are a matched pair regardless of their difference in station. He now visits six or seven times a year instead of thrice.

Allenis's father, the Duke of Teillai, died last winter, and since Allenis has taken over the reins of the Duchy, his visits have been less frequent. There are new white hairs wound with his dark, springy curls, and a new line across his brow when he frowns. The question of when he will take a wife is more pressing now, and they have talked long into the night on more than one evening. On the morning before he leaves, he rolls over to face her.

"You would make the finest duchess I can imagine," he says, his fingers tracing her hairline, the edge of her ear, the hollow of her neck. "You would manage the household, the castle, and townsfolk with the same tireless skill with which you manage your thriving business. Osthegn could be in no better hands. And I love you."

She is glad the morning sun is at her back so he can't see the sudden tears his last words bring to her eyes. Words they have never spoken to one another in all these years. She buries her fingers in the curls outlining his head and brings him close for a kiss, light at first, and then as passionate as any they've ever shared.

He breaks their embrace before it goes further. "Does that mean you will?" he asks.

Damn him for asking. For ruining this perfect relationship they have built.

She shakes her head, tears wetting the pillow it still rests on. "I can bring skill, and yes," she admits, "love to a marriage. But I cannot bring connection. Years ago you shunned Rillonna —"

"A marriage neither she nor I wanted," he interrupts.

"Nevertheless. Marrying a mere leaseholder from her duchy would be an insult that could tear the principality apart." When first she met Allenis, she knew little of, and cared less for, the politics of the nation and its neighbours. But their friendship has educated her. "You know full well you must make an alliance. Perhaps with one of your peers in Aerach, but better yet with a neighbouring principality. You know this as well as I, or else you would have asked this when your father was still alive."

He leaves in better spirits than might be expected from a man who had just been rejected, and she knows her answer is correct. "Will you take a husband?" he asks as he mounts his horse.

"I see no need," she replies, and kisses him hard when he bends down for a farewell embrace.

Saoira leans on the neighbour's paddock rail and scratches Buttercup around the base of his horns. He's a full-grown bull of seven years now, with a massive neck and muscled shoulders. He's lost the doe-faced sweetness he once had, but his coat is a richer gold than ever, shining in the Garelan sunshine. The giant red-and-white bulls and curly-haired blacks that he shares his paddock with ignore Saoira, having long ago reckoned she only brings treats for her golden boy.

She sent Reeth out with the herd this morning. Her stomach and her mind are too unsettled to give the ladies the watchful eye they deserve on the high pastures. She pulls the letter from Allenis out of her apron pocket and reads it for the third time.

Within a fortnight of his departure, a letter arrived, delivered by a ducal courier. "No longer a mere leaseholder," the letter said, and it was accompanied by deeds to the portions of land both the dairy and the creamery stood upon, with first grazing rights to the surrounding commons.

And now this letter, six weeks after that, tells her that he will travel to Rheran, in the Principality of Brandishear, this coming midwinter to betroth himself to Prince Chanist's eldest daughter.

Her hand rests on her belly, flat still but causing her no end of fatigue and missed meals. "Will you take a husband?" he asked. Does this change her answer? There are many local farmers who would take her hand, with or without a duke's bastard inside her, but none she'd want to share a bed with. Or she could visit the midwife for a tincture to abort the foetus, saving herself the worry, time, labour, and cost of birthing and raising a child.

She gives Buttercup another fond scratch behind the horns, and the last piece of turnip she'd saved him. A duke's gift is not to be squandered, no matter the trouble it causes.

§

For more high fantasy, family drama, and political intrigue set in the lands of the Ilmar, check out the spellbinding Allaigna's Song trilogy from JM Landels at Pulp Literature Press.

A SUMMER SOUP TO CURE MAGICAL THINKING

Kim Harbridge

Kim Harbridge *is a writer and editor of speculative, scary, and otherwise strange fiction. Her writing has been published in* Strange Horizons, Ellery Queen Mystery Magazine, *and* AE Science Fiction. *Her story 'Projections' appeared in* Pulp Literature *Issue 27, Summer 2020. You can find her online at kimharbridge.com.*

A Summer Soup to Cure Magical Thinking

Any soup is a summer soup if you make it in July. Any thought can be magical if the right person is thinking it. But you know all this already. Just like you know any bone will break, splinter, and stab after it has been boiled, any tears worth their salt are worth saving, and any loss that lingers as remorse is ripe for a remedy such as this one.

Serving size

This recipe will make as much soup as required, not a drop more. Do not under any circumstances attempt to double or halve.

Ingredients

- A bone, the fresher the better
- Herbs stolen from a neighbour's yard
- One onion, juicy and fragrant
- A root vegetable harvested under a full moon

Method

Gather your ingredients. Do not get confused when sourcing the first two items.

The soup starts with the bone. If you have a whole carcass at your disposal, choose the bone that calls to you, the one that yearns to be turned into something else, to live its second life. Make that bone into broth, any way you choose.

Next, strip the herbs from their stems. Strip yourself of your garments while you're at it, to prevent the stems from feeling too conspicuous. Draw the blinds if you don't want to be observed by your neighbour, who is probably out in his yard right this minute hunting whatever creature he supposes has plundered his oregano and thyme. Add the herbs to the broth. Retain the stems.

Using your sharpest knife, the one your late husband gave you on your wedding night, slice the onion into the broth. Take care not to cut your palm, but know that a drop or two of blood never spoiled a broth that wasn't sour already.

Fight the urge to wipe your eyes. What would you use, anyway? This recipe? If you've followed the instructions correctly, by now you are naked, one hand gripping a knife and the other dripping with milky onion juice. (If you haven't followed the instructions correctly, you should start over for your own good.)

Stand with your face above the broth. Let your tears season it. This should be easy after the year you've had. The memories you've worn thin since you've been alone.

Simmer until your eyes have dried.

Remember the root vegetables. Add them to the broth and continue cooking until your frustration with yourself, your fading memory, subsides.

Remove the bone from the soup. Set it aside.

Let the soup sit overnight under the moon. Sit with it if you like. Feel the warm summer air on your skin, the moonlight in your marrow.

Do not, under any circumstances, stick a finger into the pot, not even for a pinky-taste to see how it's coming along.

The next day, get dressed. Something clean, conservative, but not too funereal. Perhaps the drapey blue number your husband always liked.

Gather up the stripped herb stems, the spent bone, and the pot of soup. Bring them all next door. Tuck the herb stems back into the soil you stole them from. Stick the bone in as well. Cover with dirt, and spit twice.

Knock on the door. If no one answers, knock again and call out *anybody home?* because the soup will not keep for long.

When your neighbour finally comes to the door, bags under his eyes, reeking of sweat and sadness, tell him you're so sorry for his loss. Tell him his wife was always so kind to you, even after all that business with the homeowners' association and your chickens last year. Tell him how she was the only neighbour who came to offer her condolences when your husband passed, and that she'd brought a beautiful basket of flowers and carrots from the garden for you. It is imperative that you mention the garden, the love with which she tended it, how beautiful it grew as a result.

Wait for him to mention the ransacking of her herbs. Look shocked. Then, glance back at the plant you stole from and say something like *it looks like everything is accounted for.* If he seems upset for having hallucinated some missing sprigs, smile kindly and say he can't be expected to keep track of the comings and goings of a garden at a time like this.

Hold up the pot of soup. Invite yourself in. Do not brook argument.

Inside, fill two bowls with the soup and serve. Between spoonfuls, tell him it is not his fault. It's only natural to blame oneself when this kind of tragedy occurs — to think there must have been something one could have done to change the outcome. Tell him that you can relate.

Don't mention that the circumstances were a little different for you. Your neighbour blames himself for not saving his wife; you regret being too grief-sick to seize your chance to bring him back. Your neighbour won't have to suffer that same fate, so no need to mention it. Best not to say anything that might cause him to put down his spoon. Not when you're so close.

Serve seconds. Pat your neighbour's hand. He will find this gesture comforting.

Do not stop eating until you see the bottom of the pot or he admits there is nothing he could have done to save her. Whichever comes first.

The pot should now be empty enough to hold the guilty excess of his grief. Refuse his offers to clean it and bring it back to you later. Take both the pot and the grief with you when you go.

Retain for use in Rice Pudding to Raise the Dead (recipe on next page).

MATTAWA

DS Martin

***DS Martin** is the author of five poetry collections, including* Angelicus *(2021),* Ampersand *(2018), and* Conspiracy of Light: Poems Inspired by the Legacy of C.S. Lewis *(2013)—all from Cascade Books. He is Poet-in-Residence at McMaster Divinity College. He is also the series editor for the Poiema Poetry Series, for which he has edited more than thirty poetry collections and three anthologies. He and his wife live in Brampton, Ontario.*

Mattawa

What is unseen is sometimes discoverable
through reading the signs
                                        A half-dozen crows
startled into the air at our passing return
to the same grassy ditch

Deer remain beyond the tree line   their
conflicting instincts twitch   behind jittery eyes
                                        the forward propulsion
the uh-uh up ahead
            the pounding heart   the desire to dart
                                        the trickle of cool waters
the ugly scent of spent fuel
            the perpetual image of canine pursuit
the naked opening
                                        the whisper of tender shoots
the wide   nowhere to hide
            where warm sun through the poplars
                                        dapples their coats
that approaching whoosh   like a windless wind

hunger in the belly
that bite in the gravel
that bite in the gravel
the panic   the uh-uh-uh panic
the leap   the dash   the glisten of speeding metal

On our way back through
unscattered crows testify
I slow to see why

MAYFLIES

Liza Potvin

__Liza Potvin__ was born in France, and studied in Denmark, France, the US, and Canada. Her books include Dog Days, The Traveller's Hat, *and* Cougarman Percy Dewar. *In 1993, she won the Edna Staebler Creative Nonfiction Award for* White Lies. *Her work has appeared in* Quarry Magazine *(Best Story, 2000),* Zygote Magazine *(First Place, Fiction 2001),* The New Quarterly, Room, CV2, *and elsewhere, and was anthologized in* Outskirts: Women Writing, *and* Islands West: Stories from the Coast. *Her essays have appeared in* Descant, The Ohio Review, The Antigonish Review, Queen's Quarterly, The Malahat Review, *and elsewhere.*

Mayflies

Sarah and I met at an Indonesian vegetarian restaurant in Ubud, where our tables were so close together that getting up required begging one another's pardon. Needing to use the washroom, we did this twice, as if to certify our civility. I'm rather introverted, but I felt obliged to acknowledge her. Proximity breeds familiarity, and it seemed natural to begin a conversation about what we had ordered, especially as her dish was nearly under my nose. Like me, she was eating alone, so we smiled a couple of times before I asked her if she wanted to join me over dessert. We'd both recently arrived in Ubud. By the time our coffees arrived, I told Sarah that she was welcome to join me afterwards for a traditional Wayan shadow puppet show at the centre of town, a half-hour walk away.

Leaving the restaurant near dark didn't mean that it was any cooler outdoors than it had been throughout the day. The air was still humid and hot after the sun disappeared. Walking that evening felt like wading through treacle. On our way to the show, we turned a corner and headed toward the Sacred Monkey Forest Sanctuary. Momentarily blinded by the headlights from oncoming cars illuminating a shower of whirling particles, we stopped in our tracks at the same time.

"How can it be snowing here? We're in the tropics!" I shouted.

Blinking hard, we noticed other people shrieking loudly and backing away from the sidewalks. Long-tailed macaques careened towards us from all directions, teeth bared aggressively. To get to the papery flakes as they fell from the sky, they crawled over pedestrians, some of whom beat them back with umbrellas while others tried vainly to kick them away. A burly man said to me, "It's the mayflies they're after!" as he fled to the far side of the street.

"What are mayflies?" I blurted out, to no one in particular. I was completely focused on Sarah, who stood immobilized in fear, eyes wide in panic. Her arms were thrown up in the air as if she were under arrest.

"I hate monkeys," she muttered, leaning as if to step forward but frozen beside me while the mayflies descended upon her. A wily macaque crawled up the back of her leg to swipe at her handbag. I wasn't close enough to grab the bag. Trembling, she lowered her arms to her sides and then squeezed them to her ribs to prevent the thief from obtaining his treasure. I ran closer and grabbed her by the elbow, guiding her through the gauntlet of frantic creatures as we crossed the street towards the curb. Once we moved beyond the congestion, I looked up. The faces of drivers in cars were suspended in surprise, headlights illuminating dense ribbons of chaos in the air as the long-limbed creatures pawed at mayflies and stuffed them into their mouths. The monkeys burst beyond the boundaries of the park, spilling onto the street, swinging from telephone wires and dropping onto the heads of stunned tourists below. I pushed us both forward until we emerged at last on the other side of the mayfly storm. Sarah promptly burst into tears. Seeing her vulnerable face both pained me and endeared her to me. I did my best not to stare at her.

She was still shaking when we found our destination, where we faced a locked gate at the entrance. *Puppet Show Cancelled,* read the sign. A brief gust of wind inflated my shirt as we ran across the street and ducked into an open-air bar.

"Double vodka and soda," Sarah said to the waiter, before we even sat down. "All that for nothing." Sarah was clearly shaken. "Not that seeing a puppet show could make up for that nightmare!"

We sat for a few minutes in silence. She gulped her drink quickly and asked for another. I described to our server what had happened.

"What *was* that we just saw?"

He turned his jet-black eyes to me as if he'd finally noticed me, and then spoke quickly in flawless English.

"Those macaques are just cleaning up the streets, sir. Mayflies are born in the morning and die the same night. They have no mouths, so they can't eat. All dead." He mimed a closed mouth, his small fingers pinching his lips.

"Sex and death all in one day. Not even a good meal in between! Hardly seems fair," I said. He shrugged his shoulders, sauntered to the front desk where a textbook was splayed out on the counter, and returned to his reading. Although I was certain the mayfly storm was over, I agreed to share a taxi with Sarah back to our rooms so we could navigate the monkey zone safely. From the inside of the vehicle, the street now appeared quiet and dark. It was almost impossible to imagine the carnage that had taken place there earlier. The few macaques in sight sat sedately on telephone poles and tree limbs, fastidiously grooming one another and ignoring pedestrians.

I returned that evening to my rented room in a family compound, where I'd left a reading lamp on. My desk was littered in dead mayflies, and the mosquito net over my bed was completely covered in dark grey corpses with transparent wings.

We seldom know when we're making a memory. I forgot about the mayflies and failed to stay in touch with Sarah, even though we'd exchanged our addresses. That's the way it always is with travelling: you share an intense experience with someone and are full of good intentions to stay in touch, with promises to visit each other's countries, but it never happens. And yet on the road, you engage in the same ritual repeatedly. I once came across a small notebook of addresses and hotel names tucked away in the zippered outer pocket of my backpack, and its earnestness made me chuckle. I never stayed in touch with anyone. Kathleen says it's my one big flaw: I'm really better with numbers than with people.

I settled into work after my holiday. Life in the tech sector of the San Francisco Bay area had a certain urgency: there were long hours of staring at the computer screen followed by wild house parties and then more projects that ignored the changing of seasons. After several years, I was promoted to project manager and bought my first house. I spent most of my free time testing software in the large study that contained all my computing equipment. I also designed an outdoor kitchen modelled on the one I'd seen in my guest house in Bali, recalling the extended family rituals that had set apart village life there. I tucked the design sketches in a file folder and put it away.

Just before going to bed at night, I'd stare at the beautiful images of waterfalls on my screen saver and think about all the places I'd never visited. I no longer had time for extended journeys. All that artificial greenery on my computer was merely a visual antidote to the numbers I stared at all day. My sleep ritual involved listening to the recorded sounds of waves crashing or raindrops falling. I didn't go outdoors much to see real waves or feel the rain.

"When you get older, time will just fly by, faster and faster," my old Aunt Margaret used to say, holding up her wine glass at Christmastime. As a bored adolescent for whom time moved far too slowly, I dismissed her tipsy ramblings. But one day I heard her voice in my head and I knew she was right. I'd moved on to work in cybersecurity by the time I married Kathleen, a broker I'd met through my cousin, and we had two children in quick succession. When we bought a bigger house, I finally built my outdoor kitchen. It was stunning, Kathleen agreed. Unique.

Those early years were a blur of sleeplessness and monotony. I'm stunned when I see the photos documenting all our family birthday parties. All I remember of those events is the annual fatigue of dumping paper plates, desiccated cake, and torn paper hats into trash bags and then pouring myself a stiff drink before mopping up the sticky floor. Kathleen always reminded me that our kids were growing up quickly, that I needed to pay more attention to them. I tried to contribute to child rearing, but my efforts were minimal and we both knew it. Eventually I stopped feeling guilty about it.

We seldom used the outdoor kitchen, but I enjoyed looking at it from my office window. I imagined a feast I could prepare for guests once I found the time to organize a large outdoor gathering. Maybe a barbeque to celebrate the arrival of our next child, whom we'd determined would be our last. Kathleen had already booked an appointment for me to get snipped.

Our third child, Philip, was born with severe disabilities, and we were filled with a grief we could never fully acknowledge to each other.

"Maybe we should take a holiday," I said to Kathleen a week after his birth, hoping that a trip would lift her spirits. Of course, I got lectured about my insensitivity. Briefly I wished we'd had amniocentesis and that Kathleen had aborted; then I felt terrible for thinking that. Whiskey bottle in hand, I broke down and cried on the phone with my friend Kevin. I had no pride. I didn't care. Our dog Maisie paced back and forth between both rooms, lifting her head and sniffing the air. I was terrified that we'd be in and out of doctors' offices for the rest of our lives. Having grown up with constant illness in my parents' lives, I wasn't prepared to become a serious caretaker again. Kathleen was in the next room, also bawling on the phone, our sobs alternating crescendos between the walls.

I started drinking more than usual. Zadie and Max, overwhelmed at the arrival of their new brother, began spending more time with their school friends. We gave Philip our full attention.

"I've been taking those antidepressants, but they're not doing much," said Kathleen when I'd found her in bed after slipping home early from work one afternoon.

"I get it. I've been having trouble keeping my mind on projects at work," I told her. I crawled in beside her and knew we would both prefer to stay in bed forever. Stroking her hair as I lay beside her, I glanced at the bedside table and saw a recently framed photo of Philip, whose character had emerged slowly, gradually charming us as he grew. I was remorseful for having entertained the ideas I did following his birth. Ashamed, actually.

Kathleen went down to part-time with her brokerage firm, but by the time Philip was nine, even that became too much. His frequent outbursts were unpredictable and sometimes violent. It was a hard decision for her to give up the firm she'd helped found, but she deemed it expedient and practical. She felt resentful that the burden of caring for him fell largely on her shoulders, even though the choice to stay home was hers. I thought that bringing home the bacon was a big enough contribution, and she knew I was working hard.

Shortly after Philip's twelfth birthday, I came home to find Kathleen staring out the huge bay window in the living room, her gaze unfixed. She seemed unmoved by the beautiful trees and flowers well maintained by our gardener.

"What is it, honey?" I asked, joining her on the couch.

"It's Philip. He stinks. There's nothing else I can do." Her face was frozen in dismay.

Philip was growing into adolescence and refusing all our attempts to teach him hygiene. I marched up the stairs to his room and found him hunched over a comic book.

"Hey, buddy, how about a shower?" The room was rank with the smell of dirty socks and unwashed hair. But my boy seemed oblivious. He looked up at me and grinned.

"Sure. Just not with Mom around. Tell her to leave me alone."

Philip always responded well to me, but then I didn't have to spend all day with him. What seemed like a charm offensive to me only aggravated Kathleen further, and we agreed that we needed a full-time caregiver who could cope with Philip's spasms and tantrums.

The idea of going to Bali came from Kathleen. She'd just read Elizabeth Gilbert's *Eat, Pray, Love,* and I asked if she was having regrets about how her life had turned out. Once we started planning, I felt excited at the prospect of a change of scenery.

We decided to plan a holiday there. Zadie and Max didn't want to miss their final swim competition and wouldn't come with us, so Kathleen's sister agreed to move in to keep an eye on them. It would be a different experience travelling with Philip, and of course we'd need to find an all-inclusive hotel with full services. I'd never have imagined when I was younger that I'd travel in such dull style, but it was now necessary under our circumstances.

The mayfly memory, buried for many years, came flashing back. I told my wife about the experience in Ubud, shuddering as I remembered it.

"I can't get that weird image out of my head: this cloud of mayflies in the lamplight, while we were in total darkness. And those violent macaques swarming us!"

"Why do you raise your voice when you talk about it?" she asked, staring at me quizzically, one finger over her lips, and her other hand pointing to our bedroom door to remind me that everyone else was sleeping. "What's really bothering you?"

I couldn't answer that.

For the next week, the spectacle of that night in Ubud hovered near the edge of my consciousness, assuming Biblical proportions. At certain moments, under great stress, I could sense the mayflies fluttering on the periphery of my vision, just beyond reach. When I tried to describe it to Kathleen, she laughed.

"You're lost with the fairies again. Remember how your Aunt Margaret used to talk about fluttering at the edges of her sight? And look where she ended up! Soon you'll be losing your marbles too."

It wasn't my marbles I minded losing, just my youth. Life is too short to be wasted, they say. Lying in bed one Sunday morning, I told her about the ceremonies performed several times a day by Balinese families. "Do you know that they spend a quarter of each and every day praying to gods, every day creating those flower baskets and incense beds for all the shrines on their property? And then more for other temples too."

I described the gracefulness of the people, how their traditions marked the changing of the seasons. "Marriages and funerals are group rituals, not like ours. Wait till you see the enormous funeral pyres. Everyone wears such gorgeous clothing," I told her.

"Ha, you're still such a romantic," she sighed.

When we finally arrived in Bali, I had to adjust my view. Bali had developed enormously in the intervening years. I recalled rustic streets outside of the capital Denpasar, where a taxi driver would have to swerve around an animal pulling a cart. Even in the more developed areas closer to the beach, cars would bump along badly paved and narrow alleys twisting between a small number of T-shirt shops. But here we were, stuck in a traffic jam at ten o'clock at night, flanked by new concrete buildings that had sprung up by the side of the road. No donkeys to be seen.

Philip was squirming in the back seat, where our nanny Grace stroked his arm and sang soothingly in Tagalog. We were all sweaty. After another hour of slow-moving traffic, I felt Philip's impatience. At Kuta Beach, a large shopping centre had taken over the ocean-facing street. It was new and flashy, brandishing the names of some of the world's top designer companies on its exterior. It didn't look Balinese. We could have been in Beverly Hills. Sunglasses and ice cream outside, high-end fashion and fast food inside. All along the beach strip, international chains dominated. We might as well have stayed at home.

"Look! Pick up that garbage," chanted Philip. The beach was littered. Everywhere we saw beer-can holders with Australian or British football team logos; phone covers with the same glitzy designs we'd glimpsed in Singapore just days earlier; clothing intended to survive just as long as a holiday. Plastic bottles and wrappers dotted the beach strip. Local papers issued calls for sustainable tourism and alarming reports of water shortages and rising pollution levels. The coral reefs in the major diving centres were dying, the waters slick with sunscreen.

We enjoyed time on the beach, time away from our work, but there was little culture to explore in our brief time there. Philip was agitated constantly.

"You know, his seizures are easier to manage at home," said Grace, exhausted. It was no holiday for her either.

"I'm really grateful that we don't live in a developing country so dependent on tourism," I told Kathleen on the plane back to the States. I kept getting blinding headaches, with flashes behind my eyes.

"I'll be glad to get home, back to routine. And air conditioning!" Kathleen agreed, squeezing my hand.

Back home, I wasn't alarmed when newscasters announced that drought conditions were arriving even earlier this year; this was common during Californian summers. We turned off lights when we left rooms. We kept our showers to five minutes. We didn't let taps run. We didn't water our lawn or refill our pool when severe water restrictions came into effect.

On Saturday night as we sat on the patio, we saw a brilliant sunset that didn't fade into the night. On the radio, we heard about the fire coming closer to our neighbourhood, but, knowing that it was still many miles away from us, we slept soundly. In the morning, I woke up and smelled something burning. I thought that Kathleen must have started breakfast early for the kids. I came down the stairs in my bathrobe to see her jamming photo albums into our largest suitcase.

"How could you have slept through the emergency evacuation alert?" She didn't even look up at me. Then she was shouting.

"Get dressed now! Grab the passports. Take the whole fire safe box. We'll be waiting in the car," she yelled as I headed back up to the bedroom. My legs felt heavy as I trudged back down the stairs, out the garage door and into the car, where my family sat waiting, their anxious bodies humming like electrical wires. Kathleen stared straight ahead, distraught. She clenched the keys in the palm of her hand until I grabbed them from her and started the ignition. I had no idea where we were going.

Along the road we saw bright bursts of flame on either side that metastasized every few minutes into large flares. Wild orange particles licked the air and floated downwards, a fleeting benediction of drifting paper on the long line of vehicles. I was reminded of the mayflies: ashes bursting forth from the darkness, this time illuminated by a fierce red heat on either side of our slow-moving car. Taillights from an endless line of cars pulsed ahead of us like fireflies. A shower of ash and sparks saturated my vision. Driving through the inferno, I thought of the house that we'd spent so many years renovating and decorating: I should have fed more people around my outdoor kitchen hearth. I didn't want my life to be over. I wanted more time to look at the faces of my children, now shining in the glow of the blazing fires we passed. In the rear-view mirror, I could see that we were being chased by billowing clouds of smoke, and I had the sense that we'd never be able to turn back. The smoke made my eyes smart, and tears rolled down my cheeks. All that I cared for, the warm and breathing bodies of my family, surrounded me right now, right here. As we moved ahead, pushed together toward a horizon I couldn't yet glimpse, I leaned out the window and tilted my face toward the sky, ashes falling softly on my face.

MARTY

Kevin Sandefur

Kevin Sandefur *is the capital projects accountant for the Champaign Unit 4 School District. His fiction has appeared in* The Saturday Evening Post, The Gateway Review, *and the 2020 and 2022 Bath Flash Fiction anthologies. Two of his stories have previously appeared in* Pulp Literature*: 'Out in the Sticks' in Issue 33, and 'Floaters' in Issue 35. 'Marty' received an honourable mention in our 2022 Raven Short Story Contest. Kevin lives with his wife and two cats in Champaign County, Illinois, which is a magical place where miracles happen almost every day, and hardly anyone seems to find that remarkable.*

Marty

She first spotted him through the kitchen window as she rinsed out her morning coffee cup. He was the biggest cat she'd ever seen, but he wasn't fat. He was just, well, big. His matted fur was the colour of rusted iron at sunset, but it did nothing to hide his ribs. He was missing a hind leg, and she wondered how he managed to perch on the back-porch rail. Highlights of grey around his whiskers made him look unusually old for a feral, but mostly he just looked a mess. And hungry. He looked hungry.

There were two leftover pieces of bacon still on her plate by the sink. *Don't feed him,* she told herself. *He'll just keep coming back.* As she watched, the cat turned and looked straight at her, more or less. It was hard to tell, since his eyes pointed in slightly different directions. *He can't see me through the window,* she thought, but the cat kept staring. *Oh, well,* she finally told herself, *I'll probably never see him again.* She took the plate outside.

She saw him again the next morning. This time she had some leftover sausage. The morning after that, it was just some eggs. She started deliberately not finishing her breakfast so there would be something left for him. *It's not like it's costing me anything,* she thought.

“Why’s there a bag of cat food in our shopping cart?”

“It’s for Marty,” she said.

“Who’s Marty?”

“He’s the cat in our backyard.”

“We have a cat in our backyard?”

“That’s a popular theory.”

“Does he have a tag or collar?”

“Nope.”

“Then how do you know his name is Marty?”

“I don’t. He just reminds me of Marty Feldman.”

“You named a stray cat Marty?”

“Yes.”

“So, we have a cat now.”

“It would seem.”

“Are we sure the cat doesn’t have us?”

“How would we tell the difference?”

Over time, Marty’s appearance improved. His fur started to fill back in, and so did his muscle and fat, so his ribs no longer showed.

“Doesn’t he look good?” she asked.

He took a long look. “I guess. Healthier, maybe. But that is still one ugly-ass cat.”

“Be kind,” she said.

One morning the cat food bag was empty. “Not good,” she said. “We need to stop at the store on the way home tonight,” she called out.

“Why? What did we forget?” he asked.

“Cat food.”

“Ooh,” he said, and joined her in the kitchen. “Any scraps

from breakfast?"

"I already cleaned up."

He shook his head. "Not good."

"I know, right?" She poked her head out the back door. Marty was waiting patiently for his breakfast. "Sorry, dude. You're gonna have to wait until we get home from work." The cat stared blankly back at her. "Good talk," she said.

Marty wasn't there when they got home. "You didn't really expect him to still be sitting there, did you?" he asked.

"No, you're right. He's a morning guy. Do you think I should leave a bowl out, just in case?"

"It'll just get stale. You know how finicky cats are."

"You're probably right."

He found her staring out the kitchen window the next morning. "What's up?"

"Marty brought friends today."

He leaned over to look out the window. There were roughly two dozen cats sitting on the deck, all staring at the back door. "Does that seem right to you?"

"I don't think I have enough to feed them all," she said.

"Nor should you," he replied. "We can't have dozens of cats coming here every morning."

"What should I tell Marty?" she asked.

"Seriously?"

"I don't know, I just …" She shrugged without finishing the sentence.

"Come on, we're gonna be late. They'll be gone by tonight. Remind me to hit Redbox on the way home."

The neighbours started calling her at work around lunchtime. "What are you people doing?" asked the man next door.

"I am *so* sorry, Mr Klepke," she told him. "I don't know what's happening. They just started showing up."

The widow lady down the street wanted to know if she could keep some of the cats. "I guess that's up to them, Mrs Swanson."

When they got home that night, they paused inside the screen door before turning on the back-porch light. Hundreds of glowing pairs of eyes stared back.

"I've got a bad feeling about this," he said.

"Do you mind if we skip movie night this week?" she asked. "I'm thinking about going straight to bed and hiding under the covers."

He turned off the porch light and closed the door. "Absolutely."

The sound of the helicopter directly above their house woke them up. He strained to see upwards through the bedroom window. "Is that Channel 3?"

She turned on the television and chirped involuntarily at the live overhead shot of their backyard. "THOUSANDS OF CATS IN ST JOSEPH," read the banner across the screen. The reporter in the chopper was saying that the crowd of cats stretched as far as he could see.

They went into the family room and opened the blinds to reveal a sea of felines. "Now what?" she asked.

"Sell the house?"

"Good luck with that."

"Maybe we could get into a witness protection program."

They stared in silence for several minutes. "We're gonna need a bigger bowl," she finally sighed, and went into the kitchen to rummage through the cabinets.

"You're not seriously thinking about going out there, are you?"

"You got a better idea?"

"Yeah. Nuke 'em from orbit. It's the only way to be sure."

"They're just cats, not xenomorphs."

"Right. Nature's perfect killing machines, and you're wading out there ringing the dinner bell. What could possibly go wrong?"

"Here, hold this." She handed him the bowl they normally used for popcorn, pulled down the fresh bag of cat food, and dumped the entire contents into the bowl. It formed a giant mound in the centre and spilled over the sides. She opened the inner door to the porch and took back the bowl. "You've got my back, right?"

"Sure, Jim. I'll just be over here circling in the Land Rover while you wrestle the anacondas."

"Okay, Marlin Perkins," she said. "Just be ready to pull me back in if this heads south."

"Like Tippi Hedren in the upstairs bedroom. Got it."

She paused to collect herself. "Once more unto the breach." It didn't sound as confident as she'd hoped. "We've got this, right?"

He picked up the broom from beside the door and waved it like a polearm. "Darmok and Jalad …"

"… at Tanagra," she finished, and opened the screen door. The cats nearest the house backed out of the way, and she tentatively placed one bare foot onto the deck. *One step at a time,* she thought.

"One step at a time," he said out loud.

She took another step. *Fear is the mind killer,* she repeated silently to herself, wishing that she remembered how the rest of it went.

She could see Marty now, and the cats continued to give way around her as she moved slowly toward him. From inside the house, she could hear the reporter on the television delivering a play-by-play of her every move. She wondered what her parents would think, watching her get devoured by thousands of cats on live television. *I'm still wearing my nightshirt,* she realized.

Marty was waiting patiently. She stopped directly in front of him and slowly set down her offering. "Don't turn your back on them," came the warning from inside the screen door. "Just back straight up. Don't panic. And don't blink."

As she backed away, Marty stretched for a long, luxurious minute before sniffing at the pile of food. Then he began to eat.

When she was back within reach, the screen door opened and he pulled her inside, closing it quickly after. She hugged him tightly as the tension drained. "That was a hell of a thing," she finally said. "What are they doing now?"

They turned to look back through the screen door. Marty was still eating. The rest of the cats were just sitting there, watching Marty eat. And eat. Five minutes. Ten minutes. Fifteen. Still eating. "How is that even physically possible?" he asked.

"I know, right? Where is he putting it?"

Marty stepped into the bowl to reach the final crumbs in its bottom. Finished, he sat up for a moment to clean his whiskers, then turned and hobbled away. The other cats followed. Ten seconds later, the yard was empty.

The next morning there was just Marty, all by himself, waiting for his breakfast. She brought out his regular bowl and set it down. He sniffed it, then began eating.

"Whaddaya wanna do today, Marty? Ya wanna go bowlin'?"

He didn't look up.

"I guess not," she answered for him.

He licked up the last crumbs, sniffed the bowl again to make sure that nothing was left, then sat up to clean his whiskers.

"That was quick," she said, and picked up the bowl. Pausing in the doorway, she looked up at the sky. "The weather's starting to turn colder. Winter is coming. You want to come inside?" She held the door open.

He yawned the biggest yawn she'd ever seen, so big that she wondered if his jaw could come unhinged like a snake's. Then he stretched every single muscle individually, flexing them in order from one end of his body to the other. When he was finished, he stood and limped away.

"Well, okay then," she said.

WHEN A MAN KNOWS MUCH MORE THAN WE EVER DID

Kelli Allen

Kelli Allen*'s work has appeared in numerous journals and anthologies in the US and internationally. Kelli is a founding editor of* Book of Matches *literary journal. Her latest book is* Leaving the Skin on the Bear *(2022) with C&R Press. Two of Kelli's poems have appeared previously in* Pulp Literature, *in issues 17 and 20. She currently teaches writing and literature in North Carolina. Visit her at kelli-allen.com.*

When a Man Knows Much More than We Ever Did

Seamus carries his stories in a blood clot. Each afternoon he blesses the cockroach beneath his window and the sparrow hawk just beyond. He is not the last of the grandchildren to recite limericks before sleeping, but he was a young man when snows first covered the steeple on King Street. The sight of metal stained white arrested his steps then and keeps his pace circular now. Seamus marries a woman drawing every Saturday's bath, and he gives her bouquet to the radio altar, knobs turned to his left, antenna soldier straight. He writes his brides' names in sugar and when the ants come, they bring titles and history before spiralling back down mounds under an oak. There is a worn-out donkey grazing thistle, dreaming all day of his lamb-hide saddle and an obscured blue mountain pass. Seamus knows where the ostrich bone brush is, but he is too tired to tend a beast of such burden, even when four knees bend and wait all morning.

Speaking just one word means the throat Seamus no longer trusts will stammer a cough for hours. The end is coming for him, but Seamus is wrong about when. He is concerned for stubbornness in the Gospels and there is no way to save the pages from his stove. There is no alchemical recipe for turning jokers into queens, and the cards too, then, are food for dinner flames. The night he dies will be soon, but there is twine still to tie notes meant for the messenger of beets and milk.

His house is not quiet as it begins to fold around Seamus. Each wall takes its turn pulling downward into an envelope, sometimes a cherry-blossom crane. There will not be records in the courthouse, and acreage will abhor becoming inheritance. Whorls on his toes point to no more crimes.

When the women come to plant onion bulbs in this thickening earth, one might cinch her waist in reverence as her heel divots row after row. She was once a bride, once a bather in Seamus's vacant chapel. Even water hidden from the pond remembers its mother loch when swirled into a tub. But forgetting is longer than womb threads and the prayers of lobster clans.

What remains of one man's kingdom is a pin, lightweight and rusty feathered, disappearing into newly sown soil. None of us may understand suffering, but Seamus let his fingers dent through when he played his guitar, and we, those who walked by unaware, never even bothered to listen through the window. What do the drums say now? They say pulling the tent flaps down will make no difference. One man is just one man, and all raptures require an attention none of us is rich enough to pay.

6-MINUTE QUIZ: WHAT PERCENTAGE MONSTER ARE YOU?

Beatrice Morgan

Beatrice Morgan *is a chronically ill nature nerd and writer of speculative and historical fiction. While her body is located in a little English village amidst rolling green hills, her mind wanders deep ocean trenches, half-hidden histories, and the faerie otherworld. She has too many houseplants and just the right number of dogs.*

‹ › ⋮

Am I a Monster? Quiz!

Start →

6-Minute Quiz: What Percentage Monster Are You?

The problem with latent traits that may or may not emerge between the ages of eleven and thirty-five is I spend a lot of time wondering if I might be a monster.

It's a big deal. But also not. Rather, it isn't supposed to be a big deal, because monstrous traits emerge in lots of people (even if lots of people also do a decent job of hiding them whenever possible), but it's also not ever really mentioned. Like puberty, or menstruation, or peeing after sex: natural and normal and the sort of thing bullet-pointed on a leaflet you pick up absent-mindedly in the doctor's waiting room before tossing it aside the moment you realize the contents.

No one talks about it. You know, the fact that *lots of people are a little bit monstrous.* Which means it's disconcerting to think of confiding in anyone, even my family or friends, when I notice things changing. Shifting. I start to perceive light a little differently. I'm no longer comfortable with the rhythm of my day. My skin feels stretched tight over too many bones and misplaced flesh. It's like the body I've always lived in isn't the body I've always lived in anymore — but not by much. Nothing to explain to a doctor with the expectation of being taken seriously.

That's the other thing: it's all a bit medicalized. It's what activists and associated do-gooders say in the campaigns that people don't pay attention to: 'talk to your doctors if you're worried'.

But I'm not worried about life looking a different colour than it used to. Most of the time I'm just slightly unsettled. Occasionally I'm on edge. Right now it's 2:46 am and my bed covers are too heavy on my limbs and I'm panicking. But I don't want to talk to a doctor, so I turn to the next best thing. The internet.

How do you know if you're a monster?

The first result is

Latent Monster Traits (for Parents) paediatrichealth.org

which I hover over briefly before moving on. The second search result is

Monstrosities: Facts for Teens findafamilydoctor.com

but I'm not a teenager so I keep scrolling. The next link is more promising, meeting my extremely recent but firm criteria for a result that isn't about or aimed at kids:

Am I a Monster? 11 Things to Know If You're Questioning Your Humanity creatureme.de

I back out as the page is loading because I'm not questioning my *humanity*—the mere suggestion forms my mouth into a knot—and in desperation I open

What Percentage Monster Are You? Take this 6-Minute Quiz

I can do six minutes. I can make my lungs draw in air for six minutes; I can steady the hands so desperate to shake; I can ignore the clammy damp sticking my hair to my forehead and my pyjama top to my low back. I can do this.

1. When you encounter someone with sunken eyes, sallow skin, and prominent canines, you
   (a) want them to bite you, so you can bite them back in a mutually bloodthirsty exchange
   (b) want them to bite you, but only because it feels good, and you don't want to bite them back
   (c) want them to please go away

I read each option blankly, then read them again. This quiz is going to take a lot longer than six minutes, I realize, because I've never even thought about being bitten before—I didn't know it was something to think about.

I pick one answer at random, but the moment it is highlighted by the thick blue border, my skin prickles, like a dark cloud has sidled across the sky while I've been bathing in sunlight. Not cold, but definitely less warm. I picked incorrectly; it doesn't fit me at all.

I give myself a moment to breathe, considering the options properly this time, and when the blue highlight moves to a different answer, I know it fits.

2. When attending a bacchanal or similar gathering of drunken revelry, you

(a) experience a state of tumescence and desire for sexual contact that lasts for hours or days at a time
(b) experience physical excitement, but you only want to chat—no touching
(c) enjoy your drink and go home

There is a link to another article just below it ("Arousal Non-concordance: Know the Facts") but as much as I'd like a rabbit hole, any rabbit hole, to take my mind off my present identity crisis, I resolve to persist with the quiz. I've never been to a bacchanal, but I draw on my most bacchanal-adjacent memories (rather horrendously, my brother-in-law's bach party) and take my pick.

The posed scenarios continue. I have to remember how I felt when I spent too long staring at the flaming heart of a bonfire. Then I have to decide what I'd do if I was on an evening hike across the moors and saw dancing lights out of the corner of my eye.

7. When you spot a full moon, you

(a) feel a throbbing call in your blood to sing to her with a howl
(b) join in with howling if everyone around you is doing it, but otherwise don't bother
(c) think 'that's a lovely moon' and carry on with what you were doing

Choosing an answer never gets simpler, but it does get a little bit easier. Fun, even? Like I've blown cobwebs off a mirror I didn't realize was dusty, and the reflection looking back is crisper than I've ever known. I see myself—understand myself—with such ridiculous clarity I want to laugh. How it wasn't obvious before, I don't know. But the longer I spend in this ruminant limbo, the looser my skin feels, settled comfortably over the right amount of body.

I reach the final question. It is 3:03 am. Seventeen minutes I've poured into this six-minute quiz.

13. When you swim in a body of natural water (like the sea or a lake), you
    (a) try to stay underwater until the burning in your lungs fades and taking a breath feels possible
    (b) enjoy floating at the surface and splashing around in the shallows
    (c) get out the moment something slimy touches your toes

I remember the last time I went swimming: in an eye-stinging public pool where the urine content was the only natural thing about it. Before that was a trip to the seaside; at the recollection, a corner of my mouth curls unbidden. The final question. And I know right away which option to choose.

With quick flicks I scroll up, reading over each choice to make sure it is correct, because there is too much riding on this cringey pop quiz, and I don't want to screw it up. I change my response to question five.

Back to the bottom of the page. The inevitable conclusion has formed in my heart before I reach the SHOW ANSWER button, but I click it anyway. I want to see it set out clearly in writing. Yet the moment it appears on the screen, my throat seizes in an iron grip, and I'm panicking again. Not because it is wrong, but because it is so very right.

MY LOVE EXHALES ON THE OTHER SIDE OF THE MOON

Haro Lee

***Haro Lee** is a Korean poet and English teacher living in South Korea. Haro's work appears or is forthcoming in* Michigan Quarterly Review, Zone 3, The Offing, The Indianapolis Review, The Texas Review, Anhinga Press, *and others. Haro was the recipient of* Epiphany Magazine's *Breakout 8 Writers Prize.*

My Love Exhales on the Other Side of the Moon

The gathered body upon bed:
It desires
in a river of dried amphibians.

Its bones are the tunnelling pipes
that rise from the river's disuse
like waning moons
whose ghosts run through them now.

Come nightfall, with curtains drawn
and hearts slackened in their drum, it
feels the absence most. Without
trickle, without burst,
it burns.

THE JACK WHYTE STORYTELLER'S AWARD

Jennifer Lott

***Jennifer Lott** became a novelist in her late teens, when her author mother refused to write an alternative ending to the Animorphs series for her and insisted Jennifer do this herself. She has since completed several novels in her own fantastical worlds and created an online audio drama called* Wilzerlott. *She lives in Prince George with her husband and three children, who are a constant source of inspiration. 'Thirty Minutes to Live' was an honourable mention in the Jack Whyte Storyteller's Award at the Surrey International Writers' Conference in* 2022.

Thirty Minutes to Live

***Damn, noble death** by portal is slow.*

Anita set her phone timer for thirty minutes and took a second to make sure her doom was on track.

The braided ring of alien metal under her bed clinked quietly as it rotated. It was already projecting a narrow beam of light to a spot in the middle of her carpet. The spot was slowly widening. Only a pencil would fit through at the moment, but soon it would be human-sized, opening onto a wondrous, horrible place.

The planet Glithera hadn't always been horrible. When the portal finished expanding, she was going to make it right.

She walked out of her bedroom, leaving the door open, and faced her combined living room and kitchen.

Her basement suite wasn't well-stocked for final wishes. She spread her most expensive chocolates across her kitchen counter. Five left. She could eat one every six minutes. She uncorked the wine meant to grow old and dusty. It wouldn't age now. She'd need it to fill the minutes between chocolates.

She went to her coffee table and tapped a soft rock playlist on her laptop, letting vague sentiments dance in her ears. She switched on her smart TV, immediately hitting mute on the remote. No noise from those flashing faces. It was just the illusion of people she wanted in the corner of her eye. Silent people were comforting. Present but not painful.

She set her phone upright at the back of the kitchen counter. The countdown was set so the screen wouldn't go dark. She wanted to see the end coming. Somehow, that felt better: an appointment, not an attack.

There was a knock on her front door.

Anita hesitated. If her landlady thought she wasn't home, she'd try again in the morning. Morning would be fine. She'd find six months' rent and no tenant. She'd been a good landlady. Anita had nowhere better to leave her life savings.

The knock came again. Louder. Persistent. Not someone willing to assume she wasn't home.

She'd get rid of them quickest by answering.

She opened the door.

Her heart gave a thud.

Derek! His brown eyes locked onto her. His stubble smelled of aftershave, and his soft dark hair was damp on his forehead.

There wasn't much time to take him in. He had the nerve to start kissing her without preamble. Warm feelings went zinging through her, flushing her face. It wasn't even awkward kissing. It was the best kind, like at the height of their relationship. He'd shuffled well over the threshold, into her home, before she remembered they were very much at rock bottom.

She pulled away from him, backing up quickly to close her bedroom door. "Are you drunk?"

"Do I taste drunk?" he asked, sneaking his lips right back to hers.

She stifled a laugh as she pushed him away. "Like gummy bears. What is this?"

He swallowed hard. "I was wrong. I shouldn't have left."

Her insides went cold. "You're a little late."

"Why?" He jerked his head at the bedroom. "You got a guy in there?"

"No."

"Then why?"

"I got over you."

She knew he was processing two possible truths as he stared at her. Her tone hadn't delivered. He kissed her again, lightly, on her lips, her jaw, her ears …

She didn't move. "I mean it."

"Yeah," he said, breathing on her neck, "but you smiled for a second, so I might have five more minutes."

She savoured the inevitable tingles as his kisses grew bolder.

Five more minutes …

Her eyes strayed to her phone.

Or twenty-five?

Hell, it beats chocolate and wine.

She swept those off the counter as she pulled him back into it. She buried her hands in his hair and kissed him fiercely.

The way his arms went around her was instantly satisfying. She heard the wine glugging out on the floor. She jumped up to sit on the counter before her feet could get wet, wrapping her legs around his waist.

She felt his warm hands under her shirt. She pulled it off and threw it down. Her heart raced under hot skin that wanted his. She pulled off his shirt.

He gasped when their lips came apart. "Do you have condoms? I didn't think I'd get this far."

"Doesn't matter."

"What?" He dodged her lips, stroking her hair. "Now you want kids?"

"Doesn't matter." She pulled him in tighter.

She felt the throb of anticipation as his hands slid over all the right places …

He leaned back. "Why doesn't it matter?"

She glared. "If you make me think, this won't happen."

"Come on, I'm not sixteen. You can't threaten me with that."

"Oh, really?"

"I want to know if we're getting back together."

"If I say we're not, do you really want my clothes back on?"

But he'd stopped listening. His face slowed her flying heart rate to a death march. His grim face stared right past her to the only thing she hadn't knocked off the counter. The digital glow of the numbers seemed to stare through her skull, accusing her without words. She shivered.

"Let's catch up first, say for about"—his eyes flicked up from the phone—"an hour?"

She squeezed her eyes shut. "No."

She felt his body detach. She looked at him when she heard his foot kick the wine bottle. He started checking carpeted spots behind her furniture. The braided metal ring that opened gateways between worlds worked best on soft surfaces. It didn't do well in bright light, either. He lifted her couch to check under it.

She rubbed her forehead. "Crap, I should have got you drunk."

"Where's the portal?" he demanded.

"It's none of your business anymore."

"It's crazy! You can't do it."

"Again: not up to you."

She jumped down from the counter and found her shirt. It had fallen in the spilled wine. She put it on anyway, letting the wet spots cling to her skin.

Derek didn't bother with his shirt, but he wasn't even eye candy at this point. There was a vein popping in his neck. His throat worked. His hands shook. She couldn't stand how he got when he was upset.

"Anita—"

"I'm sick of half measures to protect the Glithrens!" she shouted over him.

"Why now? Not because we—"

"Get over yourself. I would have done the right thing eventually."

"But it would have been harder if I'd stuck around?"

She clenched her jaw. He didn't get to hear that. She wouldn't give him the satisfaction.

In all fairness, though, she'd never seen him look less smug. "Well," he said, "I'm here now. I'll make it impossible."

"How?"

"By … by pointing out a specific crisis here on Earth that desperately needs your lifelong *living* attention."

She sucked in her cheeks, loath to smile while he struggled to come up with one.

He turned away. "Give me a minute."

She watched the timer go down ten more seconds. "My lifelong attention won't solve anything on Earth."

He whirled around. "The Glithrens can fix their own problems!"

"We caused their problems."

"It was an accident!"

"Time to clean up the spill."

There was silence. Dark, hollow silence. It felt that way even with her laptop singing sweetly. She sank down on her couch, watching the muted faces on her TV screen without really seeing them.

"I've got twenty minutes. If you're not going to make them fun, get out."

She regretted her tone the moment she heard it. The dismissive cruelty.

It's still his fault, she thought bitterly. *This was so much easier ten minutes ago.*

Derek opened her bedroom.

She jolted from her trance. "What do you think you're doing?" She dashed in after him.

The portal opening on her carpet was almost big enough for a cat, but it was faltering. The braided metal that had spun in soft darkness under her bed was now spinning in Derek's palm under the glare of her desk lamp. He was loosening strings of metal in the braid, trying to pull the thing apart.

Horror crept over her, leaving her frozen, staring.

"That will close it for good," she said, half hoping the reminder would bring him to his senses. "We won't be able to fix it."

She promptly crushed her other reaction: her survival instinct that could screw over so many people with its simplicity.

He doesn't care about them, she realized, her hands curling into trembling fists. The resolve in Derek's face was like an animal's—no justifications necessary.

He glanced up. "I don't expect you to ever speak to me again."

"How do you expect to live with yourself? They've got no chance if I don't go back."

"They have warriors."

"Warriors who aren't surviving past age ten in human years!"

"They're not kids! They hit puberty way later than us. They're adult warriors too young to reproduce."

"You're making my case. If the Sukorb drains them *all* to the point that they die that young, they won't have *any* descendants!"

"They'll kill the Sukorb before that happens. They'll be fine."

"No, they won't!"

She made a grab for the spinning metal, but he closed his hand. He jumped clear as she threw herself against him. She fell forward onto her desk.

She could hear her furniture dragging even as she straightened and turned around.

Her bookcase and her wardrobe came together in a barricade. Derek panted behind them. He was boxed into the corner of her room with the portal opener. The back of her bookcase went almost to the ceiling, and so did the back of the wardrobe.

She pounded her fists against them both, screaming.

"Okay," he said, a sliver of his face looking out at her through a gap. "Keep fighting me. You can live guilt free the rest of your life. You tried. I stopped you."

Jerk!

She bent her knees and pulled at wooden ledges. She couldn't tip the bookcase over. Books weighed a lot, fine. But the wardrobe felt like a ton of bricks, too, despite its missing drawer.

Stupid heavy crap! It was too ridiculous to lose Glithera to a little thing like man muscles.

She was dizzy with panic. The details of her home swirled uselessly around her, like there was a fire and she couldn't remember where the extinguisher was.

Fire . . .

Camping! Firewood!

She dashed to her front hall closet. It had been a while, but that axe was still there. Time to chop up a wardrobe.

Derek's sliver of a face didn't even flinch when she swung at the thin wooden backing.

Glad I'm trying, are you? she thought, swinging her axe faster and faster. *Watching me clear my conscience?*

She gritted her teeth, whacking the blade beside loose screws. With a few more well-placed whacks, the whole backing came off. She pushed the unhinged drawers out the front.

Derek was gratifyingly startled. He obviously thought he had plenty of time to close the portal. The ring he'd been unravelling dropped from his hands and spun sluggishly on the carpet. He didn't dive for it in time.

She snatched it up, pinching the strands back together. The portal sprang wider as the ring spun in healthy circles between her hands. It was opening the portal as wide as she needed. One more expansion was all it would take. She sat with her legs bent over the spinning ring, the axe just within reach beside her.

Derek bent to snatch the ring.

She flipped the axe, butting the handle against his abs. "Don't even think about it."

His mouth twitched. More of a muscle spasm than a smile. "You'll have to use the other end."

"You need to leave."

"Can't do that."

"Yes, you can! You shouldn't have come!"

The portal expanded right under her legs. Her stomach plummeted as she fell infinitely further than her bedroom floor usually allowed. As she fell, she felt Derek's hand close tightly around her wrist.

"Let go!" she shouted. She felt his body knocking against her.

Then it was over.

They fell onto dusty ground. The air was fresh and cold. The sky was dark, but it wasn't night time. Before she saw a single Glithren, Anita saw the airborne monstrosity that blocked an astonishing expanse of blue sky.

Whenever it inhaled, the enormous Sukorb covered Glithera's sun. It inhaled with its black nostrils, each of which could have held a dozen houses. When it exhaled, its wings curled down just enough to shine with sunlit edges. It could have looked like a manta ray save for the gaping void of a mouth that was its reason for living and its long-range weapon. This mouth could have swallowed a town, but it didn't need to. It neither swallowed nor breathed. All it ever did was suck.

It took no time at all for the Sukorb to sense her presence. She felt its suction seize hold of her, sure as a fist around her heart.

It wouldn't be that quick. The beast was making a leisurely meal of her life force.

It didn't hurt as much as she thought it would. Her skin prickled all over like pins and needles. Her head grew heavy and sore.

She could still feel Derek's hand on her wrist. His grip was tight, but shaky. His head drooped, and she knew at a glance that he was feeling everything she was. The Sukorb was draining them both.

Her eyes smarted. Her sore head made muffled protests. If only she'd done this earlier, just a little sooner, he'd still be safe at home …

She strained to keep her eyes open, to see the Glithrens one last time. At first, all she could see were their luminous arrows shooting up at the Sukorb's nostrils, disappearing uselessly in those depths.

Then she saw the warriors hovering nearby. Glithrens couldn't fly like the Sukorb, but even in infancy they could float a foot above the ground. They propelled themselves like motorboats on the air, without any visible sign of propulsion.

They had bald, glowing heads with eyeballs dotted all the way round. No necks. Short torsos that ended like bee stingers. Their four glowing hands on each of their four long arms were always quick and clever. The arrows flew from those hands without bows. Glithren hands, themselves, possessed the talent. Their professions were more inborn than learned.

The one Glithren on the battlefield who couldn't shoot arrows from his hands was a doctor. Anita could tell by the way his hands glowed: white light with an overlay of skeletal shadows. X-ray hands.

The doctor glided right up to her face and smiled sadly. Glithren mouths were expressive with smiles and frowns, but not with speech. They didn't have voice boxes. Like legs, those were wholly unnecessary. Their telepathic language was better than a universal translator. It had shocked Anita on her first visit. Who knew minds could communicate without shared words? She heard her own version of what they said echoing in her brain like they'd bounced it off the walls of a canyon.

"We did not expect to see you again," the hovering doctor said to her. *"We warned you what would happen if you returned."*

She bobbed her heavy head in acknowledgment. "Sorry I took so long."

The doctor's front-facing eyeballs were fixed only on her, but she was sure he was allowing Derek to hear him. Most Glithrens assumed she and Derek were mated for life, since anything less in romance was difficult for them to comprehend. It was proper etiquette to keep him in the loop.

"The Sukorb has hungered for your poisonous life force all this time. It seems

to have mistaken your mate for an extension of you. Is his life force equally tempting and poisonous?"

"Sounds right to me," said Anita.

She tried to turn her head to glare at Derek. Her teeth rattled in the pulling wind. She could hear his teeth rattling beside her. His grip on her arm was weakening. He was going to die, too, and she couldn't even muster the energy to tell him what an idiot he was!

Arrows flew faster. The Glithren warriors seemed to be inspired by the diversion. Or perhaps revitalised, because the Sukorb was no longer draining life out of any of them. The bodies on the ground were warriors who'd fought too close for too long. They were being wrapped and carried away by hundreds of Glithrens with the hand talents of fast travel. One set of arms jetted the traveller back to the nearest city while the other set carried a fallen hero.

The funerals would keep coming. The arrows were not piercing anything.

Just keep drinking me, Anita thought, cutting her unwanted help right out of the equation. *Keep going, you greedy bastard. Drink faster.*

She grinned through her rattling teeth, because she could feel the enormous wobble at the other end of her killer's straw. It was filling its belly with exotic, foreign life forces it wasn't equipped to handle. It was getting very sick.

The arrows stopped. The silence in the absence of the Sukorb's breath was stunning.

It was falling from the sky!

The fast-travelling Glithrens stopped ferrying the dead and instead jetted the living out from under the falling mass.

Anita's heavy eyelids flew wide as she realized she and Derek were also being propelled out of harm's way.

The vibrations as the Sukorb hit the ground were tremendous, knocking Glithrens into helpless somersaults through the air. Anita lay sprawled, panting, confused.

"Is it dead?" Derek breathed by her ear.

She got slowly to her feet, watching the Glithren doctor ascertain that very thing. He took a good five minutes to hover over the entirety of the monster's internal organs, using his hands to scan it thoroughly.

His next thoughts were so loud Anita was certain he was talking to neighbouring cities. *"The humans' poison has saved us! The Sukorb has been destroyed!"*

Anita's head filled with the cheers of countless citizens. Voices she never thought she'd hear. Four-armed hugs broke out everywhere. Glithrens danced to music that strummed from luminous musician hands. She watched as smiling, floating faces filled the sunlit battlefield.

"How did it die?" she asked. "I thought it had to drain me completely."

"Double poison ended it before it could complete its feast," said the doctor.

Derek turned cooperatively to accommodate the doctor's X-ray hands as they read his body. Anita watched the glow travel down her wine-stained T-shirt. Each additional breath in her lungs felt too good to be true. No news could be bad.

The doctor's hands dimmed. His eyeballs gave them equal attention, his mouth a solemn line. *"Half your lives have been torn from your bodies. Your stolen years cannot be restored. You will each die when you reach the halfway points in your natural lifespans. It will happen instantly."*

His serious tone was soon drowned out by the cheering crowd.

Anita couldn't blame them. She wanted to think, but it was hard amid the clamour of intruding voices. For a while, she couldn't even tell if any of them were speaking to her.

She finally caught one specific question. Did she and her mate want to stay for the celebrations?

"No, thanks," she whispered. "Home."

Guiding hands brought them back to the portal. It felt like being carried to bed after partying too hard: gentle, forgiving.

They fell upwards.

Anita found herself in her messy bedroom, taking in its unremarkable chores. It felt stranger than draining her future for a Sukorb's demise to know that she could think about picking up clothes or buying a new wardrobe.

Maybe a defence mechanism, she thought, *so I won't focus on ...*

She listened to Derek breathing beside her. His fingertips brushed hers.

"That's fifty, right?" he said casually. "I'm dropping dead on my fiftieth birthday? Probably. Better not to know exactly, I guess."

She edged her gaze towards him. If he was covering up a bigger reaction, she'd lose sight of it the moment he looked back at her.

"I'm sorry," she said, dropping her eyes before he could.

He took her hands. "I had no plans for after fifty."

"I had no plans for after today."

It suddenly felt like a lot. Life going on. She felt her throat constricting. If she was about to burst into tears, it was one hell of a delay. There was no need to cry now. She swiped at her eyes, embarrassed.

Derek didn't make it worse by trying to get information so he could fix it. He just put his arms around her.

She rested her head on his bare chest, the tightness in her

throat easing. It was like they'd never been apart.

His closeness started to feel like a question. She decided to hazard a guess and answer it.

"I still don't want kids," she said. "And now any kids you have will lose you when they start college."

"I don't want kids. I want my nieces and nephews. I want you."

She met his eyes and believed him. It was enough to overwhelm her again. The idea that life would not only go on, but that the person she loved most would be in it.

He wasn't the best face reader.

"I know you think I'm selfish, and you'll remember you're mad at me in a minute. There's just no one else to hug and you're a bit shaken up. I'm not making any assumptions, but if I could at least—"

She kissed him. "Assume we're together until the next time you choose me over an entire alien race."

He stroked her arms. "Could we just not meet any more whose planets have hidden life force–sucking monsters waiting for clumsy humans to wake them from their comas?"

"I'm okay with that."

She smiled through her tears as she held him close. Life felt anything but stolen. Years be damned. There would be so many more minutes.

THE BUMBLEBEE FLASH FICTION CONTEST

THE 2023 BUMBLEBEE FLASH FICTION CONTEST

Like bees in a bountiful garden, we were delighted by the spectrum of this year's entries. Here's what final judge Bob Thurber had to say about the shortlist: *"There's much to admire in these stories, some curious, some amusing, a few beguiling tales, all of them entertaining and fun to read. I wish to thank all of the finalists for their superb efforts."*

Winner: 'Reap What You Sow' by Alex Reece Abbott
Honourable Mentions: 'Vulnerability, Now and Then' by Soramimi Hanarejima, and 'Tourist Trap at the End of the World' by KT Wagner

Bob praised the winning story as *"a curious work replete with captivating images,"* and he offered *"approving nods"* to the (unranked) honourable mentions.

Congratulations as well to the shortlisted authors:

Finnian Burnett
Chelsea Comeau
Soramimi Hanarejima
Mamie Potter
Tyler Pure
Alex Reece Abbott
Alan Sincic
David Stephens
Mitchell Toews
KT Wagner

Thank you to Bob Thurber for once again lending us his expert judgement and comments, and to all submitting authors for sharing your words and supporting *Pulp Literature.*

New Zealander–Irish writer ***Alex Reece Abbott*** *was honoured with Flash Frontier's Summer Writing Award. Alex is also an Irish Novel Fair, Northern Crime, Arvon, and HG Wells prize winner, and a Penguin Random House WriteNow finalist. Her work is widely anthologized, including in* Best Small Fictions, Bonsai: Best Small Stories from Aotearoa New Zealand, *and* Heron. *Two of Alex's short stories have appeared previously in* Pulp Literature, *'My Brother Paulie, a Domestic Space Odyssey' in Issue 19, Summer 2018, and 'Alphabet Soup' in Issue 20, Autumn 2018. Find her on social media @AlexReeceAbbott.*

KT Wagner *writes speculative fiction in the garden of her home on the west coast of Canada. She loves to knit and is a collector of strange plants, weird trivia, and obscure tomes. KT graduated from Simon Fraser University's Writers Studio in 2015, and two of her stories have appeared previously in* Pulp Literature*: 'Cabin Fever' in Issue 24, Autumn 2019, and 'Winter's Flower' in Issue 29, Winter 2021. She organizes writer events and works to create literary community. KT can be found online at www.northernlightsgothic.com and @KT_Wagner.*

Ever yearning to be spellbound by ideas of a certain fanciful persuasion, ***Soramimi Hanarejima*** *often meanders into the euphoric trance of lyrical daydreams, some of which are chronicled in Soramimi's neuropunk story collection* Literary Devices for Coping. *Soramimi has work in* The Dillydoun Review, Reed Magazine, *and* Outlook Springs, *as well as* Pulp Literature *issues 17, 28, and 35. Visit Soramimi at CognitiveCollage.net.*

PULP
Literature
The Bumblebee Flash Fiction Contest
Deadline: 15 February
Prize $300
The Magpie Award for Poetry
Deadline: 15 April
Prize $500
The Hummingbird Flash Fiction Prize
Deadline: 15 June
Prize $300
The Raven Short Story Contest
Deadline: 15 October
Prize $300
Enter today:
pulpliterature.com
/contests

Reap What You Sow

(after *In the Distance,* a painting by Andrea Kowch)

BY ALEX REECE ABBOTT

I have seen your expression too many times before, in other places, on other women's faces.

You stand at the kitchen table of a desolate American farmhouse, dry-lipped, a flush on your cheeks, daring to dream while you work.

Need bread.

Knead dough.

Sift flour.

Stretch gluten.

Egg-wash loaves.

As the new day dawns, there's a storm brewing somewhere in the Midwest.

It's sultry, already too hot. You have pushed the windows wide open, and the gauzy curtains float in the prevailing westerly, and the breeze catches tendrils of your wilding Medusa hair.

Cut a cross in that cob like Mama showed you, let the devil out.

Under that brooding, bruised sky, the men sweat in the fields, reaping the wheat, racing to beat the tempest. His scythe is a rusting iron crescent above his shoulder, his redundant braces dangling, limp at his slim hips as he swing-swing-swings, immersed in a restless, golden sea.

Under the glowering sky, he harvests, his blade slicing the air in graceful arcs, wheat rippling in the breeze. And from the corner of his eye, he sees you, knead-knead-kneading. If his nostrils weren't filled with dust, he could smell your bread baking.

If he wasn't trying to beat the storm, he could sit in your kitchen, drinking coffee. If he had money, he could leave the acrid-rubber smell of stink bugs behind and he could share the fresh, clean air with you, swap tales and dreams with you.

If his eyes weren't stinging with salt-sweat, he could enjoy the view in your kitchen. If the rain would hasten, his hands would be free and he could help himself to a fat slice of your fresh, warm loaf, sweet and sticky with your strawberry jam.

If he had his time over, he could stroke your wilding hair again.

You swat a pestering horsefly. Moses, the hungry tabby, yowls over spilt milk, and with a flick of his curlicue tail, he leaps to the windowsill, chasing some demon, real or imagined, leaving a trail of white pawprints at the scene of the crime.

Knead, knead, need, need. More.

You turn your back on him, turn your back on the field, on that flaming bitternut hickory that burns but is never consumed by the flames.

You stand in Mama's kitchen, alone with your unwelcome news, gone gone gone.

Cut another cross.

From the fields, a voice carries on the wind … where will you go now … where is your milk and honey … where is your Canaan? You wipe your hands on your apron and you wonder who will lead you out.

Too many times before, in other places, I have seen that distant expression on other women's faces. Deer caught in the headlights of your future, a strange resignation in your eyes, and yet you are not consumed … you shall be whatever you shall be.

Tourist Trap at the End of the World

by KT Wagner

From her perch on the wall, the old woman known as Cybil sets aside her knitting to greet the gathering of hopeful clients and study the goods they hold up as potential payment. She's particularly looking for sturdy colourful yarn, romantic novels with happily-ever-after endings, and dark chocolate.

Cybil's a tour guide—one of a handful of early explorers who managed to tether themselves to a rare stable spot along the black shale-and-limestone rubble wall separating the rift from the rest of the world.

The rift's a dangerous place. With a tour guide, the fatality rate is around five percent—about the same as on an average day anywhere in the remaining habitable areas of Earth—but it's eighty percent for those broke and desperate enough to approach on their own.

The dead bodies vanish. Nothing's ever recovered, but rumours persist that some survive, passing through the oozing, jelly-like membrane to emerge unscathed into a utopia on the other side.

The rumours are wrong but, like most good stories, contain a kernel of truth. It's possible to accidentally tether to the membrane, but it changes humans beyond recognition.

Cybil spots several hefty tomes with promising covers. As twilight falls and the lanterns above her flicker to life, she glances around at her knitting. It covers every nearby object, including the base of the lanterns, several folding chairs, an old tent frame, and various pieces of driftwood hauled in from who-knows-where.

She teases free half a dozen spiralling chains of yarn and directs them toward those tourists who, in addition to books, carry other desired goods. A heart-shaped box of chocolates here. A skein of magenta wool there. Her heart skips a beat—there's a slim volume of love poems. She avoids looking directly at faces—doesn't want to know them. Conveniently, they're all well-bundled against a bitter cold that no longer affects her.

Her chosen approach. Several others loudly pray or, worse, start to keen and beg. Some have camped here for weeks. It takes time to purge the unwanted ones with seemingly random accidents.

By appearance, Cybil is the oldest among the guides. The others tell her she looks the same as when she arrived decades ago. Back then, the other guides were withering—not enough tourists to sustain them all.

She realized that more than the rift's spectacle and mystery was required to draw sufficient tourists and their offerings. The guides cannot survive an untethering, and they hold this secret close.

Cybil relayed to the guides stories of long-ago visits to Niagara Falls, Ontario, when the river still flowed. Tourists came to see the falls, but also to challenge it. Much like the rift. She paused, then ended with a flourish. "And they poured their wealth into the surrounding casinos, museums, and tourist traps." Wealth today is scavenged.

The guides created an amusement park. The not-dead work the attractions in exchange for sustenance. None can speak, few appear human, but most are still humanlike, and if they occasionally eat a tourist, well, the guides regularly disclose updated mortality rates.

Cybil leads her group down the far side of the slope; her knitting trails behind her. It's dark now, and she warns them to watch their footing as they head toward the sulphur light.

A waxy fortune teller cackles an unintelligible prophecy. A swarming mass motions them to try their hand at ring toss. Cybil lengthens the tethers to her charges, gathers their offerings, and suggests they run along and have a little fun.

She's convinced herself the newest attraction is her long-lost husband, miraculously returned from the other side of the rift. She knows she's succumbing to the lure of the impossible, which eventually takes everyone, but her logical brain cannot compete.

Only the top half of his body extends from the ooze. Ear-like hooks protrude from either side of what might be a face. It has the lumpy appearance of a dying mushroom. Only the hair looks human: rich copper curls. Jacob had copper curls. Or he did when he was younger. And maybe his name was Justin.

It doesn't matter. His carnival show convinced her. Between two appendages he clutches a flat sieve with wooden sides. Into it go the books. He shakes and shakes until words fall out below, reforming into sentences as they drift through the membrane and disappear—too quickly to read, but she's sure they speak of love.

She offers the chocolate. His extremity envelops her as she leans in.

Vulnerability, Now and Then

by Soramimi Hanarejima

After she gets in the car, we look at each other, and I can tell from her expression that she can tell from my expression that I can see through her. And, wow, can I ever—to the point that I can make out the mangoes and avocados of a fruit stand framed by the car window behind her. For a long moment, there is only charged eye contact and her lips pursed at my eyebrows raised at her diaphanous appearance—the dour line of her mouth seeming to chastise me for seeing something I shouldn't have, though of course there's no way I'm not going to notice that some perceived threat has made her involuntarily turn translucent.

"The interview?" I ask—because it's possible that on the way over a car swerved in her direction or a dog barked ferociously at her.

"Yes, the interview," she says. "Which is ridiculous because I'm overqualified for this position, and really I should be past this whole thing by now."

No one is ever past their evolutionary heritage, but of course I'm not going to say that.

"I can't go in like this," she declares. "The hiring manager will know how easy it is for *everyone* to tell when I'm feeling vulnerable. Even if he takes me at my word that this rarely happens, he's going to worry that it'll happen at some inopportune, high-stakes moment."

"Well, let's go anyway. Maybe you'll feel better," I say, hoping my words sound genuinely optimistic. "And we can try doing some deep breathing when we get there."

Miraculously, she doesn't protest, so I start the car. Cool air wafts from the vents and caresses my forearms, providing relief I didn't know I needed. I pull away from the sidewalk, and neither of us says anything while we make our way down block after city block. Thankfully, there's little traffic, and I only have to stop for red lights. Every time I do, my ears perk up with the expectation that she's going to tell me to just take her home.

But she doesn't and eventually says, "This shouldn't be happening. I'm so much more confident now. To the point that the vestigial invisibility has hardly been a problem. Practically non-existent compared to before. Remember how in middle school this would happen all the time? When I had to recite poems for literature class or, ugh, work in a project group with a classmate I had a crush on?"

"I remember," I answer, though what I want to say is she's always looked good that way—like this—airy and kind of magical. But telling her is unlikely to help.

"That was so embarrassing. Now this is like back then all over again. And I'm back to wishing I hadn't gotten this from Mom's side of the family. Which is a terrible feeling to have because I know that without it, there might not be that side of the family. And I am grateful that our distant ancestors could become invisible in those jungles full of predators. That must have made their lives much easier, but what's left of that ability hasn't made my life any easier."

For a while, she just stares out the windshield, then quietly says, "I just want to be proud of how this connects me to my family history, and not worry about how people react to it."

I look in her direction to give supportive eye contact. But I've barely gotten a glimpse of her when I'm stunned by her almost normal appearance.

"Look in the mirror," I blurt, then turn my attention back to the road.

She flips down the passenger-side sun visor and angles the mirror toward her.

"Whoa, what happened?" she murmurs.

"You went from being upset that the translucence would cost you the job to being appreciative of it."

"You think that's it?"

"I have no idea what else it could be."

Then it's back to silently pressing on toward the interview, me tentatively hopeful, occasionally glancing at her—still nearly opaque, scrutinizing her reflection.

When we're about halfway there, I tell her, "Focus on the appreciation, and let's see how this turns out."

In my peripheral vision, she seems to nod in agreement. Reflexively, I check the clock, and of course we're going to arrive well before the interview starts. She always budgets plenty of time for getting from one place to another, so she has plenty of time to be grateful.

THEN AND NOW: AN ASD COMIC

Matthew Nielsen

Matthew Nielsen, *known online as Nuclear Jackal, was born in Wales, went to University in England, and eventually moved to Canada, where he now spends his free time writing comics and honing his skills. Matthew's collaboration with Minna Hakkola, 'The Endless Drop', appeared in* Pulp Literature *Issue 22. And his solo project 'Houses' appeared in two parts in issues 31 and 32. He's still working away on* Toni & Aberdeen, *a graphic novel about two time travellers who live in a deserted 2003 Vancouver. For updates and more, you can find them (and Matthew) on Instagram or Twitter @nuclearjackal.*

LET'S COMPARE A TYPICAL DAY IN MY LIFE TO VARIOUS POINTS IN MY PAST.
DAY BEGINS.
WAKE UP.
Ding!
BRUSH TEETH.
GET CHANGED.
PREPARE A PACKED LUNCH.
AT ONE POINT IN MY CHILDHOOD, I WOULD ONLY EAT A HANDFUL OF DIFFERENT KINDS OF FOOD. THE VAST MAJORITY OF MY DIET CONSISTED OF NUTELLA SANDWICHES.
NOM
nutella
Chocolate bread!
I MEANT 'CHOCOLATE SPREAD'
IT MIGHT SOUND LIKE BAD PARENTING, BUT ALMOST ANY OTHER FOOD WAS COMPLETELY REVOLTING TO THAT CHILD.
NOWADAYS, AFTER YEARS OF SLOWLY EXPANDING MY PALATE, I WILL TRY ALMOST ANY FOOD, AND I EAT MANY DIFFERENT KINDS.
OATMEAL
GIMBAP
KOTA
CABBAG
I ONLY STARTED EATING CABBAGE FOR THE FIRST TIME LAST YEAR.
MY PARENTS KNEW I HAD *SOMETHING*, BUT IT TOOK UNTIL I WAS ABOUT 12 YEARS OLD BEFORE I WAS OFFICIALLY DIAGNOSED WITH ASPERGER'S SYNDROME,
A FORM OF A.S.D. OR AUTISM SPECTRUM DISORDER IN THIS CASE.
I'VE MET A FEW PEOPLE WITH ASD WHO REFUSED TO DRINK WATER AND WOULD ONLY DRINK ORANGE SQUASH, OR IN SOME CASES PEPSI.

PUT ON SOME SHOES.
I COULDN'T TIE LACES UNTIL I WAS ABOUT 12. MY PARENTS ALWAYS HAD TROUBLE FINDING VELCRO SHOES THAT FIT.
I LEARNT HOW TO TIE THEM IN BOARDING SCHOOL.
IT DEPENDS ON YOUR SOURCE.
IT DEPENDS ON THE DEFINITION.
IT DEPENDS ON WHEN THE STUDY TOOK PLACE.
THE WORLD HEALTH ORGANIZATION STATES 1 IN 100 CHILDREN HAVE ASD.
THE CDC STATISTICS VARY FROM 1 IN 150 TO 1 IN 44 DEPENDING ON THE YEARS.
THERE ARE VARIOUS LEVELS OF SEVERITY, WITH MULTIPLE RANGES OF POTENTIAL FOR IMPROVEMENT.
This way, Davey.
SOME WITH IT CAN REMAIN IN NEED OF A LOT OF SUPPORT EVEN UNTIL AND THROUGHOUT ADULTHOOD.
SOME HAVE THE POTENTIAL TO IMPROVE, BUT DO NOT GET THE SUPPORT THEY NEED.
OTHERS HAVE BOTH THE POTENTIAL AND THE SUPPORT.
CHANGED AND WITH MY LUNCH PACKED, I GRAB MY COAT AND HEAD FOR THE DOOR.

GOING OUT BY MYSELF.
IT WASN'T UNTIL THE AGE OF ABOUT 17 THAT I WAS ABLE TO START DOING THAT CONSISTENTLY.
I WAS TERRIFIED OF GOING OUT ALONE. I GREW UP IN A ROUGH TOWN, THERE WERE OFTEN VANDALS.
I HAVE MUCH MORE CONFIDENCE NOW. THE FEAR IS GONE BUT SOME LEVEL OF STRESS IS ALWAYS PRESENT.
NOW I TAKE THE BUS.
ONCE AGAIN, I DIDN'T START USING PUBLIC TRANSIT UNTIL I WAS ABOUT 17.
I THINK MOST OF US DISLIKE USING BUSES.
IF I HAVE A SEAT, IF I HAVE A BOOK, IF I HAVE SOME MUSIC, I CAN PUSH MOST OF THE STRESS AWAY.
I START WORK AT THE DAY JOB.
MY FIRST FULL-TIME JOB WAS WHEN I WAS ABOUT 23 YEARS OLD. THEY FIRED ME 3 MONTHS IN.
I'VE BEEN WORKING AT THIS JOB FOR A FEW YEARS NOW, AND THEY TELL ME THAT I'M ACTUALLY PRETTY GOOD AT IT.
MY FIRST JOBS ALWAYS HAD MUSIC PLAYING IN THE BACKGROUND, BUT I'M EXTREMELY PICKY ABOUT MUSIC.
I NOTICED FROM TELLING MY COLLEAGUES ABOUT IT THAT IT AFFECTED ME MUCH MORE THAN IT AFFECTED THEM.

THERE ARE DIFFERENT TRAITS THAT SOMEONE WITH ASD COULD HAVE ANY NUMBER OF.
EXAMPLES INCLUDE:
SO THAT'S WHAT I DID LAST FRIDAY.
NOT MAKING EYE CONTACT
GLAD YOU HAD A GOOD TIME.
RESISTANCE TO CHANGES IN ROUTINE
WED
·AIRPLANE CLUB
·BURGERS
THURS
·CHORES
·CURRY
GOOD.
WED
·CHORES
·BURGERS
THURS
·AIRPLANE CLUB
·CURRY
This is not RIGHT!
NOT HAVING ENOUGH EMPATHY
HAT YOU SAID WAS MEAN.
WHY?
HAVING TOO MUCH EMPATHY
THAT MUST HAVE BEEN SO SCARYYY!
WELL, IT WASN'T QUITE THAT BAD.
REPETITION OF WORDS OR PHRASES
"LAUGH IT UP, FUZZBALL."
HEH,
"LAUGH IT UP, FUZZBALL."
HYPER SENSITIVITY, AND THEREFORE POTENTIAL DISGUST OR DISPLEASURE OF CERTAIN TOUCHES, SOUNDS, SMELLS, SIGHTS, TASTES AND/OR APPEARANCES OF THINGS.
A VERY KEEN INTEREST IN A PARTICULAR TOPIC
OF COURSE, WHILE THE M1919 BROWNING WAS A .30 CALIBER MEDIUM MACHINE GUN, THE M2 BROWNING WAS A .50 CALIBER MACHINE GUN, ALSO KNOWN AS 'MA DEUCE' AND WAS WIDELY USED AS A VEHICLE WEAPON AND FOR AIRCRAFT ARMAMENT.
HEADING HOME.
I WALK PAST SOME CYCLISTS.
KADMAN CONVENIENCE
I DIDN'T LEARN HOW TO RIDE A BICYCLE UNTIL I WAS ABOUT 16, MOSTLY BECAUSE I WAS TOO SCARED TO GO OUTSIDE BY MYSELF.
I'LL TAKE THE TRAIN.
A MAN ASKS FOR SPARE CHANGE BECAUSE HE 'LOST HIS WALLET'.
I FELL FOR THIS WHEN I WAS FIRST LEARNING HOW TO USE TRAINS. NOW I'M A MUCH LESS TRUSTING AND MORE SKEPTICAL PERSON.
ALWAYS BE VIGILANT.

I DIDN'T FIND A SEAT TODAY SO NOW I'M A LITTLE MORE STRESSED. MY HEADPHONES AREN'T WORKING.
I CAN HEAR EVERYONE TALKING.
I CAN SEE EVERYONE MOVING.
I CAN FEEL PEOPLE PRESSING UP AGAINST ME IN THIS CRAMPED TRANSIT.
I USED TO HAVE A LOT LESS PATIENCE.
THE STRESS WOULD BUILD UP, THEN COME OUT IN AN EXPLOSION OF VERBAL AND PHYSICAL AGGRESSION.
THESE EVENTS GRADUALLY DECREASED DURING MY BOARDING SCHOOL YEARS WHEN I WAS 13-16 YEARS OLD.
THEN THEY BECAME PURELY VERBAL.
NOW EVEN SHOUTING IN ANGER OCCURS A LOT LESS OFTEN.
ONCE OR TWICE IN THE PAST FOUR YEARS.
I UNDERSTAND THE RISKS, THE HARM, THE PERSONAL SHAME.
MY ANGER BECOMES INTERNAL.
THEN IT BECOMES SADNESS
THEN IT EVENTUALLY FIZZLES AWAY.
BUT IT TAKES A LONG TIME. I STILL PREFER THAT TO HARMING OTHERS.

I ARRIVE HOME.

MY BOARDING SCHOOL THOUGHT THAT I WOULDN'T BE ABLE TO GET INTO UNIVERSITY, BUT I SHOWED THEM.

I WAS LATER TOLD THAT I WAS THE FIRST ONE IN THAT SCHOOL TO PASS A G.C.S.E. (IT'S AN ACADEMIC EXAM AGES 15-16 TAKE IN THE UK).

I STARTED LIVING INDEPENDENTLY WHEN I WAS ABOUT 19.

I WENT ON TO GET A BACHELOR'S DEGREE IN ILLUSTRATION AT UNIVERSITY.

FOR EVERYONE, THERE'S SO MUCH THAT WE DO NOW AS ADULTS THAT WE COULDN'T DO AS CHILDREN.

NEUROTYPICAL

A.S.D.

FOR SOME PEOPLE WITH ASD, IT CAN BE A CASE OF SLOWER DEVELOPMENT.

WE MIGHT TAKE A WHILE TO CATCH UP, BUT WITH PATIENCE SOME OF US CAN GET THERE.

OTHERS MAY TAKE LESS TIME.

OTHERS MAY TAKE MORE.

DETERGENT FIRST, THEN FABRIC SOFTENER, THEN SWITCH TO THE 'WARM' SETTING...

SOME DON'T HAVE THE POTENTIAL TO GET TO THAT POINT.

I STILL FEEL REALLY UNCOMFORTABLE IF I LOOK PEOPLE IN THE EYE.
IT MAKES ME FEEL LIKE I'M NAKED OR EXPOSED OR SOMETHING.
I HAVE AN ODD WAY OF EXPLAINING THINGS SOMETIMES.
YOU'RE RE-VISITING IT SO THAT MEANS YOU'RE GOING BACKWARDS AND NOT PAST THE 'START' TILE.
YOU COULD'VE JUST SAID 'GO BACK'.
AND IF PLANS CHANGE AT THE LAST MOMENT, IT CAN REALLY MESS WITH MY COMFORT ZONE.
ACTUALLY, WE'LL GO ON TUESDAY INSTEAD OF TODAY.
WHAT!
WHEN I WENT TO A FAMILY CHRISTMAS GET-TOGETHER LAST YEAR, I WAS TOLD JUST AS I ARRIVED THAT SOMEONE I DIDN'T KNOW OR TRUST, ESSENTIALLY A STRANGER, WOULD BE JOINING US.
NORMALLY I COULD HANDLE IT, BUT THIS WAS CHRISTMAS.
IT FELT LIKE EVERYTHING HAD GONE SOUR.
IT WAS LIKE ALL THE MUSIC HAD GONE OFF-KEY.
ALL THE EXPECTATIONS HAD SHIFTED.
I FELT VERY UNCOMFORTABLE.
I FELT ANGRY.
I FELT I HAD TO REMOVE MYSELF FROM THE SITUATION.
SO I LEFT.
I SKIPPED THE GET-TOGETHER THAT TIME.
I EVENTUALLY COOLED OFF AND WAS ABLE TO THINK ABOUT IT WITH A CLEARER HEAD LATER.
BUT RIGHT THEN AND THERE, IT WAS TOO MUCH.

I'M STILL LEARNING.
BUT THANKS TO MY FAMILY,
THANKS TO THOSE IMPERFECT YET HELPFUL ORGANIZATIONS AND COMMUNITIES,
AND THANKS TO ALL THE PATIENT, ASSERTIVE, AND CARING PEOPLE I'VE MET,
I'VE BEEN ABLE TO DEVELOP AND LIVE INDEPENDENTLY.
SOME FOLK WITH ASD ARE LUCKIER,
SOME AREN'T AS LUCKY.
EVERY FEW YEARS, IT'S LIKE LOOKING BACK AND REALISING HOW MUCH OF THE WORLD YOU COULDN'T SEE.
This person cares.
This person's in pain.
Children don't know any better.
SOMETIMES IT'S SAD.
SOMETIMES IT'S SCARY.
BUT IT'S ALSO SORT OF WONDERFUL THAT WE CAN CHANGE AND IMPROVE OURSELVES.

STELLA RYMAN AND THE CURSE OF YOUTH

Mel Anastasiou

Mel Anastasiou *writes the Fairmount Manor Mysteries, the Hertfordshire Pub Mysteries, and the Monument Studios Mysteries. Winner of a Literary Titan Gold award and longlisted for the Leacock Medal, Mel is also the author of two illustrated thirty-day workbooks on story structure: the steampunk-themed* The Writer's Boon Companion *and* The Writer's Friend and Confidante. *For news on published and upcoming new works, visit her website, melanastasiou.wordpress.com.*

FAIRMOUNT MANOR

Stella Ryman and the Curse of Youth

Octogenarian sleuth Stella Ryman returns for her thirteenth adventure with Stella Ryman and the Curse of Youth. *When Thelma Hu is placed in an ambulance and Stella fears she'll never see her friend again, faking a stroke seems like a good idea. But now Stella is heading towards one hospital and Thelma to another. Undaunted, Stella will stop at nothing to track Thelma down and bring her safely back to Fairmount. You can find the first two full-length books,* Stella Ryman and the Fairmount Manor Mysteries *and* The Labours of Mrs Stella Ryman, *at pulpliterature.com and from most booksellers. Book 3,* Stella Ryman and the Search for Thelma Hu, *comes out in 2023 from Pulp Literature Press.*

Stella unbuckled her seat belt and moved to the right along the back seat of Riley's car. Once settled, she fastened her belt. From here she could keep Riley in her line of sight. Riley was proving to be something of a darter in driving style, and she had never respected these swift in-and-out-of-lane drivers who put everybody's nerves out of whack just to save a moment's travel. Back in her driving days, she had quietly enjoyed passing a seething darter forced to wait at a left-hand turn.

Stella peered out of the back passenger window at the moving city, an exceedingly grand view when compared with Fairmount Manor's sponge-painted walls and wood-tone doors. She had once known these roads on the city's west side well and now observed a few changes in the expensive section of town they were passing through, mainly pretty houses fenced for demolition. Still, the ornamental cherry trees shaded the streets the way they'd done every May while she'd been among the living and working. She felt a little like an astronaut returning from space, stunned by the relativity of time. She'd been gone for only three months but felt long forgotten by the world.

She reminded herself that she must try to appreciate the drive. Her mother had been of the generation that enjoyed a car ride, especially on Sundays. If Stella hadn't been so worried about Thelma, she would have enjoyed this ride far more. She asked Riley the time, and he told her ten thirty. She could hardly believe how little time had passed since breakfast with the Board. Now here she was, on her way to hospital, driving in apparently the opposite direction from Thelma's ambulance. Stella's fake stroke, meant to allow her to join Thelma in the ambulance, had failed, and the sense of moving farther and farther away from her friend in this time of need sent up a flare of panic inside her. Before anything else, she had to narrow the distance between them. She told herself not to show her distress, for it wouldn't help her with Riley. He could be friendly, and he might do a person a favour if it was in his interest; apparently, he liked to be liked. But he was not kind.

Stella said, "I'm feeling much better now." Was she? Stella took inventory. Heart beating at an appropriate rate, breathing consistent; everything else was gravy.

"Good news," Riley said. "You can tell the doctors when they check you out."

"I don't think I need to go to hospital after all." She felt the urge to apologize, but if there was anything one learned in eight decades on this planet, it was not to grovel before an unkind person. "Let's go back to Fairmount, shall we?"

"Can't do it. You've got to be checked out, my beauty."

Stella silently acknowledged his charm. "I don't think there's a thing wrong with me."

"Let the doctors do their jobs. That's why they get the big bucks, right?"

"Yes, of course," she said. *Doctors and lawyers and entrepreneurs, oh my.* A thought struck her. Thelma's ambulance had driven off in the opposite direction from Riley's car, but many drivers, especially those who drove for a living, had arcane knowledge of vastly differing routes around the city to reach certain destinations. "Do you think that Thelma might possibly be on her way to the same hospital we're going to? Perhaps the driver has taken an alternate route?"

"Sure, could be," Riley agreed cheerfully.

A careless reply. Nonetheless, he might be right. All things were possible, or else how was Stella out of Fairmount Manor and sitting in the back seat of Riley's car? Furthermore, at the start of the day she'd not had a penny in her pocket, and now since rich, elderly Vaughn's gift, Stella had wads of money. Even at eighty-two, one's life took unexpected turns.

Riley swerved into the left lane, back into the right, and swung over again. The traffic on Granville slowed then stopped short. Riley cursed, nipped between braking vehicles into the right lane, and turned into a parking lot.

"Are we stopping?" she asked.

"Nope. This parking lot leads into a back lane," he said.

He steered a hard left that swung Stella sideways in her seat, against the door. The turn onto a side street brought the nose of the car up against a temporary no-entry barrier. Riley huffed and backed into a private driveway, nearly hit a boat trailer, and swung around to dive down another lane. He turned right on a residential street, right again, thumped over a speed bump, and on the third right turn met the same no-entry barrier again from the other side.

"What are they doing with the traffic flow around this city?" he said. "I'm getting mad, and I don't like to drive mad."

Stella said, "Let's take a moment to get our bearings."

"I know where we are," he said.

"I don't." She did, actually; she had known a learning assistance teacher who lived on this street. "But if we don't stop a moment, I'm afraid my blood pressure will go through the roof, and things might end badly."

Riley pulled over to the curb, put his elbow round his seat, and regarded her closely. "Your colour is good," he said.

Now look who's the hobby doctor, Stella didn't say. "Let's chat just for a minute. Calm me down."

"Chat about what?"

"Well, this is a very nice car." Stella touched the seat cover. The stitching was ripped and the piping well worn, but it appeared to be real leather. "What make is it?"

Riley's expression brightened. "It's an old Saab, quite a great car if you know anything about older models. It's equipped with one of the early computerized systems, actually."

"You must have sold your pretty SUV, then?" Stella asked. "It must not have been easy to give up a luxury car even for a classic vehicle like this."

Riley nodded. "I'm saving my pennies—want to take the kids on a road trip when school lets out. Give Cheryl a break."

That was unexpectedly responsible of him. Was it possible a family man's heart beat inside Riley's shiny exterior? Perhaps he was something like the tough kids she had sometimes taught, the ones who only wanted to read books on racing cars. She had noticed that doing this sort of student a favour went a long way. She remembered the battered copy of a book on the 24 Hours of Le Mans she'd given a tough boy to keep. It had made a new child of him.

What might she give Riley? What would he like? The question was easily answered. She took a twenty-dollar bill out of the sheaf of Vaughn's money she had stuffed in one pocket and pretended to pick it up off the floor. "Did you lose this? I found it under my foot just now."

Riley reached over the seat to take the bill from her. His smile shone in his handsome face. "Money is magic, isn't it? I tell my kids, if they ever find some money, they can make a wish."

He pulled into the street, made an illegal U-turn, and the Saab was back in traffic and heading south again. The car passed a series of bright facades of mostly fast-food places.

Stella frowned. "Make a wish on money? What a pretty thought. Well, what do you wish for?"

"Gas in the tank! I'm running low. But we'll make it to the hospital, never fear."

"That sounds like a wasted wish to me, since neither of us really wants to go there."

"I guess so, but then I'm not the one who found the money. You found it, Mrs Ryman, so you get to make a wish."

"I wish to turn around and go back the way we came."

Riley's eyes met hers in the mirror. "Now, there's a wasted wish if I ever heard one. You shouldn't use up a wish wanting to drive back to Fairmount. That will happen anyway, after you see the doctor and get some tests done."

Stella sighed. This was the second time today she'd been asked to make a wish. It might even have been the second time in her life. "Well, then, I wish for …" She thought about all the things she'd missed at Fairmount. Hamburgers. Her handbag. Her collection of Colin Dexter's *Inspector Morse* novels. But no. If she were going to play with magic, she felt a duty to ask for the grandest and most unlikely outcome. "I wish to be younger."

"Don't we all! How much younger?"

Don't be greedy, Stella. "Thirteen years."

"Done." Riley laughed. Did he mean it to sound mocking? Stella studied the passing buildings until a traffic light paused Riley's car outside a pub.

Riley nodded towards the bright green-fronted facade. "That's the best pub in the lower mainland," he said. "They pour their Guinness slowly and know their correct temperatures."

"I've never seen so many shamrocks on a building, even in Ireland," Stella said. "I prefer a crisp lager myself, but when I travelled there I saw the pubs with a few old fellows drinking their breakfast Guinness."

"They say Guinness drinks like a meal."

"I'll bet the pub serves coffee. Maybe we could go in and get a cup." And maybe she could talk Riley out of checking her into the hospital.

Riley peered ahead towards the apparently static red light. "Are you trying to get me fired, you temptress? Anyway, I have a rule: I never order coffee in a drinking establishment. I'd have to order a beer. And then who would drive? Anyway, look: the pub is closed until eleven. "

"Too bad. I'd like a beer." Stella was surprised to find that her statement was true. She also wanted a bag of salt-and-vinegar chips to go with the beer. She remembered the tang of vinegar against her tongue, and the full round saltiness of the potatoes. As a child, she had put chips in her sandwiches when she could get away with it. She remembered the crunch of chips against lettuce and cheese, and the soft sweetness of the bread, which contrasted with her mother's hard look when she saw what Stella had done to her sandwich. Tanis Marie Seton was not one to alter a recipe. Stella smiled. "A beer in the middle of the morning? I'm imagining what my mother would say."

"Your mother?" Riley glanced at her in the mirror. "Is your mother still . . . ?"

"No, of course not. She died many years ago. But her opinions on drinking beer live on."

"You can buy me a brew some other time, then." The light changed at last. Riley drove through and darted between two cars in the left-turn lane.

Stella looked back at the pub. The sign on the door did read closed, but even so, a woman stood in the window with a pint glass in her hand. The reflections of shining shamrocks and the whisking shadows of cars on the window glass obscured the details of the woman's appearance beyond her narrow frame and long tangled hair. Stella wondered whether Mad Cassandra Browning might not have expanded her haunting territory. Possible, but unlikely.

A break in the oncoming traffic sent the woman in the window out of sight as car after car turned left in swift arcs.

Riley swerved left with the rest. Stella had hardly taken breath before he turned left again, drove into a covered drive, and set his brake.

"Here we are," Riley said.

To the right of the Saab, the road leading across the bridge and downtown flashed with sunlit vehicles lined up at a red light. To the car's left, the hospital's glass double doors slid open, and a uniformed medical worker exited and walked off along the highway, for lunch or maybe the end of a shift. Above the doors, a large backlit sign read *Reception, Drop-Off Only.* Stella thought of the old fairy tale, *Mr Fox.* The sign over Mr Fox's basement door had read *Abandon hope, all ye who enter.* She could easily picture those very words under *Drop-Off Only.* Furthermore, Riley had the same sort of slick good looks Mr Fox was said to have.

Riley put the car into neutral—he was hard on the gears, Stella noted without surprise. He rested one hand on the steering wheel and turned to address her. "I guess I'd better take you inside."

"The sign says *Drop-Off Only.* Shouldn't we park somewhere else?"

"I want to get you in line at emergency."

"But this isn't an emergency. Look, the sign says *Reception.*"

"Oh, for god's sake." Riley grimaced. "But maybe they can check you in here and you'll avoid the emergency wait. Dr Terry did phone ahead, but I don't know exactly how it all works. I'm sure I can leave the car here for a little while without any problem."

Stella peered at the glass doors and the big plate-glass windows to either side of the entrance. She saw a queue of people inside, one of them a man in a uniform that had nothing to do with health care.

"There's a police officer inside the lobby. You'll have to drop me off and find short-term parking or else likely get a ticket." Stella heard her own steady tone of voice and marvelled at it, because the adventurous heart that still beat inside her thrilled at being out on her own in the greater world, even if it were only a hospital lobby and just for the few minutes it took Riley to find parking. But another part of her—the institutionalized part that had spent three months at Fairmount, plus the part that had shut herself into her house and watched box sets of *Ironside* and *Mary Tyler Moore* for a year before checking herself into Fairmount—wished faintly that he'd refuse to leave her alone in the hospital.

While Riley idled the engine and peered through the windows, apparently considering his parking options, Stella watched a droopy-trousered elderly fellow limp through the sliding glass reception door and turn towards the main road. He was not quite as old as Stella was, but she was clearly a better walker. If that fellow could go to the hospital on his own, why couldn't she? Wasn't she the woman who had thought nothing of ordering five thousand dollars' worth of books to support curriculum and student interests over the course of an autumn term, of reorganizing library shelves for a more efficient layout of information, and of designing units of study for her research skills program? Or was she a mouse?

Was she a craven, irreversibly institutionalized rodent?

Two cars pulled up behind Riley's Saab, so silently that they almost seemed suspicious, like creeping footpads approaching from behind. Of course, they were electric vehicles. Was it only six months ago that she had considered buying one, had imagined gathering courage to leave her house and drive boldly to the supermarket and the liquor store? To a movie! But she hadn't done it. She had not valued her opportunities for independent travel, and now they were lost to her. She reminded herself that regret peeled no potatoes, that what was done was done, and at least she was no longer the television-watching hermit she had been a few months before. Now she was a sleuth, with a job to do and friends who counted on her for help. Today she must follow—no, pursue!—Thelma. And even though this particular hospital was almost certainly the wrong hospital, it was not impossible that Thelma had arrived here after all. For amateur detectives such as Stella lacking backup and surveillance vehicles, it was vital she not bypass any arena worthy of investigation.

The two cars idling behind the Saab let out their passengers and drove around Riley's car. Both vehicles followed an arrow indicating long- and short-term parking. The patients they'd decanted onto the walkway made their way to the reception door, one with help from a younger person and one, limping, on her own. A police officer appeared momentarily in the open door, glanced at the Saab and down the street. He moved back inside, and the big entry doors closed behind him.

Riley said, "I just feel like Mrs Warren would say it's better to leave the car here and go in with you."

"She won't like it much if you incur a parking fine. Unless you plan to pay it?"

Riley said, "Like hell I do."

"Then, when a no-parking area is this well policed, you'd better park somewhere legal." How on earth would she be able to investigate the hospital with Riley at her scut? "As well, you're low on gas. What if you go and top up the tank?"

Riley bent down to pick something up off the floor. Stella leaned forward to see him place a slim sheaf of papers on the empty seat beside him.

Stella said, "If that is my medical paperwork, I'd better take it in with me. Go and get gas before you park. There was a station near that Guinness-pouring pub of yours, just round the corner. Maybe you could have some coffee."

In the rear-view, Stella saw Riley's eyes brighten, perhaps at the thought of coffee. Or gasoline. Or even the pub.

He handed her the paperwork. "I'll hurry back," he said.

"Please, take your time." Stella set her papers down on the seat and unclipped her seat belt. She opened the passenger door and got herself up and out onto the sidewalk. Another car pulled up behind them, and Riley drove away with the back door still open. Stella called, "Oy!" and he stopped. She slammed the door shut for him. No sooner had he driven away than she realized that she'd left her medical paperwork in his back seat. She shrugged. She was not here for treatment, after all.

The hospital loomed before her. Stella straightened her fleece jacket and walked towards the entrance.

The reception door glass was well pasted with stickers reminding folks to have medical papers ready and hands washed, to phone this or that crisis number, and not to bully staff or engage in violent behaviour. To Stella these messages were refreshing, even stirring; after three months of Fairmount Manor's inane and insulting posters banning residents from climbing stairs and taking baths, Stella welcomed rules that applied to everybody, young and old.

The doors parted and she passed into the reception foyer. This area extended in a wide rectangle of ordered spaces, rather like a parking lot if the chairs were cars. The big streetside windows cast a generous light across the waiting area. The seats were perhaps two-thirds full of patients and accompanying friends or relatives, most engaging with their phones. Stella noted a single receptionist behind glass at the intake kiosk. This might have been a recipe for a long wait, but a queue of only six patients waited on painted footsteps for the mother and son at the kiosk to finish their business there. Behind Stella, the doors whisked open and two women, the younger supporting the elder, walked past her and joined the line, bringing the total to ten. Stella knew Riley wanted her to wait for him, but she was feeling a very human desire to join the queue. She checked the window to see whether Riley was approaching and, turning back, accidentally locked gazes with the police officer. She smiled at him, and he nodded. *Nothing to see here, Officer.*

She took her spot in line and gazed about her. How interesting a person would find the people waiting in this room depended entirely upon how long that person had been trapped in a down-at-heel care home. A woman in a seat near the queue wore a camel-hair coat that matched its owner's hair. She opened her top-grade red leather handbag and rummaged inside it. Stella remembered the fiendishly expensive handbag she'd bought herself the year she retired. It had been a sort of going-away present to herself, and it coordinated with the rolling travel bag her fellow staff members had given her. She'd taken these with her overseas several times in her sixties, trips she'd enjoyed mostly on her own, although once she'd signed on for Petra with a group of retired teachers. She remembered the line-up at Petra in the heat, and how she had hated the delay. It seemed she had evolved since then, because today she was enjoying herself, standing and staring as the poet William Henry Davies advised the world to do. Enjoying, in fact, the view from the queue.

The windows offered a panoramic vista onto the busy road beyond, and Stella thought of Riley on his quest for coffee and gasoline. Her own quest was trickier, for she had to investigate Thelma's possible presence at the hospital without revealing the fakery of the stroke that had brought her here.

Beside the kiosk, the police officer and a nurse chatted quietly. Inside the kiosk, the receptionist paid close attention to the teenaged boy who spoke at length, holding his arm close to his chest, while his mom hovered, interjected, and corrected him. Stella couldn't make out their words, but she didn't need to; Stella had been in that mother's place a few decades back. Her daughter Junie had taken a bad tumble while ice skating. Stella remembered the blood stiffening Junie's flesh-coloured tights, and how Stella had felt compelled at the hospital to command help and healing from all possible sources. This mother and son confab no doubt meant Stella's wait would be a long one, and judging by the sighs and shifting from one foot to another in the line-up, she was not the only one to have deduced it. The elderly woman in front of Stella leaned on her younger companion. She met Stella's eye and smiled a tired, but bright-white, smile. Stella was aware that there were some advantages to false teeth in old age, like whiteness and easy access for brushing, but she remained grateful to her long-dead dentist, an early advocate of flossing.

Stella told the older woman, "I'm happy to save your place if you'd like to sit down."

"I was going to offer you the same." The woman nudged her younger companion. "You have nobody to lean on, but I have Sharon here."

Sharon grimaced. "Aunt Bethie, I should have thought of that. What if I hold both your places? You two ladies can go rest your feet."

Stella glanced downwards. She noted the younger woman's swollen ankles above worn suede shoes.

Stella said, "Thank you so much, but I'm not tired."

"Don't be silly, dear," Bethie said. "We're all tired, aren't we?"

"And the whole world has sore feet," Sharon added. "I've been standing on mine a few years less than you have, so I'm happy to stay in line. Please, go and rest yourselves."

"Listen to the experience of youth," Bethie said.

"That's funny," Stella said, "because I'm sure it was the other way around when I was younger."

"Everything was simpler then, wasn't it?" Bethie said. "Now Sharon's the only one who can operate my television set."

Sharon laughed. "My nephew taught me. He's six and sick already of turning on devices."

"It's tough to be young," Stella joked, thinking of her grandson Derek and his impatience with unsavvy elderly users of technology. She'd never have been able to watch all those box sets of seventies television shows without his phoned-in guidance.

Stella offered Bethie her arm, got her comfortably seated near the woman with the expensive handbag, and returned briskly to the line-up where Sharon stood wiggling her toes in her shoes. Stella guessed this exercise would bring little relief to Sharon's sore feet and swollen ankles.

"Sharon, how do you do? My name is Stella Ryman. Please go and sit with your aunt."

"I couldn't," Sharon said. "It wouldn't be fair. I'm only sixty."

"The curse of youth. It isn't fair, is it? Anyway, I'm only sixty-nine," Stella lied recklessly. After all, she had wished to be thirteen years younger. "And you'd be doing me a favour, letting me do you a favour."

Sharon sighed, said thanks, and left the line-up to join her aunt. Stella felt a tap on her shoulder. An elderly fellow behind her said, "As you're only sixty-nine, would you be willing to watch my spot too?"

"Happy to," Stella said.

The woman now ahead of Stella, since Sharon and Bethie had left the queue, tossed Stella a wishful look. Stella jerked her head towards the seating, and after that, the last four behind the teenager and his interjecting mother at the kiosk took quick advantage and followed the others over to the chairs.

"They ought to have a number system," a young fellow with both knees bound up with tensor bandages muttered from behind her.

"There's a little screen up there for appointments, I'd guess, but it looks like it's out of order. I don't mind holding your place. Do go have a seat."

He hobbled off, and Stella found herself standing all alone in the middle of the floor. Despite William Henry Davie's well-known poem, standing and staring was not what one could call a conventional delight in the modern world, and she had not forgotten the urgency of her quest to find out where Thelma had been taken. But impatience had never moved a queue, and it was so long since she'd stood among people she didn't know, in comfortable anonymity, that she let herself relish the moment. She hoped that Riley would take his time gassing up and parking the car. She willed the woman—still insisting on something beyond the call of medicine for her son—to carry on indefinitely, like a good mother should. Stella felt a youthful sunniness of spirit, for she was up to her favourite brand of mischief, the kind that hurt nobody and thus was acceptable even to career educators like herself. For nobody could deny that among the crowd were several people who actually believed Stella was sixty-nine years old.

While the mom ahead spoke her volumes to the receptionist, Stella remembered how in earlier times she would have taken a book from her handbag and passed the time reading. Since she had no handbag and thus no book, she mused upon the poet William Henry Davies, and then upon Wallace Stevens, who wrote that he was the world in which he walked. Today in the reception queue, Stella was the world in which she stood. She was also an amateur sleuth with a keen intention to ask subtle yet probing questions of the receptionist when she reached the head of the line.

Meanwhile, she decided to practise her sleuthing. She set herself to take inventory of her surroundings. In front of her, by the kiosk, the police officer accepted from the nurse a brown waxed bag with what must have been lunch inside. She wondered at a police officer being stationed in a hospital reception area: was his assignment because of some kind of a crime wave, or was this simply police outreach in the community? Whichever it was, the police officer did not appear to be tense or even very alert, and there was some serious legal-medical flirtation going on now at the kiosk, but there was no way to know why he was here without … Stella cast her mind back to *Ironside* … listening to a police scanner, so she moved on with her observations.

To her left, scattered around on the waiting room chairs, a number of old folks dozed, hands on chins or heads tipped back, mouths open. Among them lounged a youngish mother in tight stretch pants and black bucket boots worn to grey at the seams. The outfit was not attractive, but Stella, in her fleece suit, felt she must not judge anyone who chose comfort over style. The woman in stretch pants had with her a little girl who wore a red hoodie that lent her a storybook air. The child swung from side to side on her mother's chair back, and Stella followed the girl's gaze back to the police officer eating his sandwich.

For anyone who has spent decades in an elementary school, sandwich smells must resonate strongly, and Stella was herself beginning to feel peckish. She hoped that Riley had bought himself a mid-morning sandwich. Perhaps he would even bring her one, if miracles happened among us, and he thought of it. Stella's stomach growled, and it struck her that all institutions counted out the last hour of the morning by the multiplying odours of sandwich fillings. Fairmount Manor certainly did. And at the school where she'd taught for so many decades, noontide burst from every child's brown bag or lunchbox. Here, the police officer by the kiosk, demonstrating good courting form, was eating his sandwich slowly and gazing at the nurse, who was bent over a tablet, tapping at paperless paperwork.

Meanwhile, the mother had worked through her son's issues and they'd left for the seating area. One by one the receptionist dealt with the others until at last she concluded her dealings with Bethie and Sharon of the swollen ankles.

"Step right up." Sharon waved Stella to the kiosk window. But the receptionist held up a hand to wait and picked up her phone.

"Stella, thank you for holding our place in line," Bethie said. "You're the angel in this waiting room."

Sharon nodded. "I can't thank you enough. Sometimes it feels like I've got cranky puppy dogs instead of feet, chewing away down there."

"You're very welcome," Stella said. "I'm happy to help your feet any day."

"I hope we see you again, Stella," Bethie said. "Are you often out this way?"

Stella grimaced. "Not often, no."

"Gosh, we were lucky to meet you."

The receptionist hung up her phone and nodded to Stella. "Good morning. Services card?"

Medical services card. Intake papers. Stella had left her Fairmount Manor medical paperwork on the back seat of Riley's car, the same car Riley had driven off to gas up and park somewhere on hospital grounds. She stole a glance at the reception doorway in case Riley was for once where he might have been helpful. But of course he was not. And anyway, she didn't want to show her paperwork for two good reasons:

1. She had no wish to be admitted to hospital, for that would put the stopper on her search for Thelma Hu.
2. Her paperwork showed her true age, which was not sixty-nine.

"Er, I've just realized that I don't have my number and the papers from my ..." She eyed Sharon and Bethie, who were listening to this exchange. "... papers from my doctor, but I think my driver has them, and I don't see him yet."

Sharon groaned. "You're going to have to go to the back of the line again. That's really unfair. Can she come right up to the front when the papers arrive?"

"Depends on the length of the line-up," the receptionist said. "And how disagreeable everybody is."

"Maybe you could find Stella's information on the computer," Bethie suggested.

The receptionist asked, "Name? Date of birth?"

"Meet my hero. Her name is Stella Ryman," Sharon said brightly. "And she's sixty-nine."

The receptionist turned to the computer. Stella's true age would soon be revealed, and she steeled herself for the embarrassment of having her birth date read out. How the Greek Chorus would delight in seeing her caught out, she reflected wryly. And even Thelma would chuckle if she knew of Stella's little white lie. Chuckle with sympathy? Stella sighed. Probably not. *Rightly* not. How she missed Thelma. She yearned to know whether the ambulance had brought her here.

Stella waited for the receptionist to finish typing and reveal her age and circumstances. *Resident of Fairmount Manor Care Home.* It was very much like being one of the soldiers in *The Great Escape*, seconds away from recapture. She vowed not to let them admit her into this hospital. They'd never take her alive. She smiled to herself: a Steve McQueen smile.

The receptionist looked up from her keyboard. "I don't have a record for you."

In the silence that followed the receptionist's statement, Stella felt inspiration's hand upon her shoulder. She asked, "What about Thelma Hu?"

"What's Thelma Hu got to do with anything?" The receptionist's eyes softened into something dangerously close to pity. "Aren't you Stella Ryman?"

"Yes, but … I'm very sorry." Stella scrambled to cut a logical path to a cogent question. "My mind was wandering, and I'm afraid I wasn't clear. I'm hoping to visit a Miss Thelma Hu, if she's here. Here in your hospital."

The receptionist frowned.

"Or any hospital," Stella added hopefully.

"You don't need a services card to visit a patient." The receptionist peered upwards at Stella.

Stella felt certain that her cover was finally blown. Next would be the phone call back to the Stalag—or rather, Fairmount Manor—and the disappointment in Sharon's and Bethie's eyes when they heard her real date of birth and saw Stella clapped into the gyves of old age and driven back to captivity.

Sharon asked, "Can you find out on the computer where Thelma is?"

"What family name again?"

"Hu? Thelma Hu?" Bethie said. "Was that it?"

"H-U," Stella spelled out. "Thelma is a resident of Fairmount Manor, and her hip was quite seriously hurt."

"No, I see no records for a Thelma Hu," the receptionist added. "And an elderly patient with hip problems would normally be sent downtown."

"Thank you very much indeed."

Downtown. There was only one important hospital downtown. Stella took the result of her investigation, chewed it, and swallowed it down.

Sharon and Bethie walked with Stella over to a seat in the waiting area. She had stood in line for at least half an hour. Riley ought to be back soon, his car gassed up and Stella's medical papers in hand. When that occurred, she supposed that all would be revealed to the receptionist, Sharon, and Bethie. It would happen soon, but not yet.

Sharon checked her watch. "They told me Cardiac is running late today, and we've got an hour's wait. I could eat a walrus, actually, and it's getting on for lunchtime."

Bethie nodded. "Let's get a sandwich in the café downstairs. Stella, will you join us?"

"I'd like to, certainly, but …" But …? What was stopping her? Only a creeping sense that the longer she talked with these two nice, unsuspecting women, the more certain it was they would find out she was lying to them. Still, she wished wholeheartedly to join them for lunch. To order a sandwich—no! Not a sandwich, she'd had nothing but sandwiches and packet soup at midday since she'd arrived at Fairmount. Sandwiches be damned. She supposed that it was too much to hope for a café to carry her preferred lunch selections from long ago, *viz.* patty melts and cottage cheese with pineapple chunks. But quiche? Yes, there might very well be a slice of quiche. *Pastry beneath the egg and cheese filling,* she thought, *and possibly bacon.* And, lest she forget, Vaughn had gifted her with a pocket's worth of paper money. She could buy a whole quiche. A dozen quiches. Every quiche in the city. "In fact, I will."

"Let's go before noon hits and we're lined up out the door," Sharon said.

Bethie added, "I'd bet my sister's cat you've had enough of line-ups, Stella."

"You'll win that bet," Stella joked, just like anybody who wasn't trapped for the rest of her life in a care home. "And a good thing, too, because what would I do with your sister's cat?" She thought of Dottie and her illicit cat, Percy, back at Fairmount. And of the Rose Corridor women, the Greek Chorus, and Theo. She swallowed. Always Theo.

Stella nodded.

"Hurray," Bethie said. "It's a treat to have you join us."

"This way," Sharon said.

Stella moved to follow. But what if Riley returned and didn't find her where he'd left her? She imagined the alarms, the blared announcements over PA systems, and her public disgrace. She said, "You two go on."

"What is it? We'll wait," Sharon said.

"No, you go ahead and order. I'll try to join you later. Please."

Sharon gave Stella a hug, and Bethie squeezed her arm. They moved off, and Stella watched them go, as grateful for the sudden affection of strangers as for the fact that the two women wouldn't witness her reunion with Riley. How long did she have until he returned to her? As long as it took him to find gasoline, coffee, and a parking spot.

But at least Stella had discovered the hospital where Thelma had likely been taken. And until Riley arrived, it was her privilege to stand in the sunny reception area, with freedom in her gullet, and an appreciation of time and place that likely exceeded everyone else's.

To all the seated visitors, the police officer, outpatients, and staff behind glass, it was a day just like any other under the aegis of the health system. But Stella felt keyed up. Here in reception, as she never had done at Fairmount, she perceived the ephemerality of belonging with these strangers in the greater world. Here, windows opened to the pavement spreading outwards into the gasping traffic. She imagined the air above the roads, coloured by collective exhausts and the blended breaths of a large city's inhabitants. Just for today, she was a part of this population. Today must be enough for her, because she couldn't stay in reception forever. And maybe she wouldn't get to eat quiche or visit that nice-looking pub they drove past on the way to hospital, where she thought she saw Cassandra Browning, of all people. Then again, maybe she would. But of one thing she was certain: if Riley came and tried to check her into hospital, he'd find himself in a fight. In the meantime, in this period of calm before his return, she might as well continue to reap the pleasures of independent anonymity. For this might be the last opportunity she ever had to breathe in the sights and sounds of a place away from Fairmount, as if she were taking in a grand bazaar on a senior's tour. She noted

1. music over the speakers, a jazz mix that would have suited a coffee shop;
2. the magenta bobble-wool jacket draped over a woman's shoulder;
3. the receptionist, attending to the line of visitors and patients; and
4. an old fellow in baggy trousers, seated with his empty pockets hanging open and his zip fly puckered and pilled.

Stella took a seat near the door Sharon and Bethie had left through, whence she could watch the entrance in case

Riley drove by. She smiled at the woman with the camel coat that matched her hair, who was still waiting with admirable patience. The woman took off her coat and hung it off the back of her chair so that it covered the red leather handbag Stella envied so.

Also still waiting, but without the same placidity, was the young mother in stretch pants and bucket boots engaged in following her daughter protectively around the waiting room. Stella noted the padding under the stretch pants' rear, which she identified now as protective cushioning for bicycle riding. She gave the mother extra points for environmental as well as parental responsibility. Just so did Stella used to follow her own daughter Junie around the park where she played. However, Junie had been a well-behaved paragon compared to this little girl in the red hoodie. The child tore around the waiting area at a pace no grown athlete could match. Stella marvelled now, as she'd always done, how children's short legs moved with swift power, light as a bird, muscles firm as a fish.

The little girl darted up and down the aisles, put up her red hoodie and took it down, brushed with her shoulder the top of the empty-pocket man's grey fringe of hair, knocked the camel-coat woman's red leather handbag off her chair, and then ducked behind the bobble-jacket woman. At last her trailing mother appeared to lose energy, stopped still in her bucket boots, and walked towards the doorway. Two cars pulled up, and new patients and family members climbed out. The police officer, now near the door, stood aside to let them through.

The stretch-panted mother stepped aside to let the new patients and their small entourages pass. Once they'd cleared the door, she stared around the waiting room and called, "Maxie?"

Patients and visitors around the waiting area straightened a little in their seats.

"Where are you, Maxie?" The woman spoke in loud, worried tones to the waiting area at large. "It's my daughter. She was here, and now she isn't."

Everybody craned and twisted. Stella looked at the spot where she'd just seen Maxie hiding behind the woman with the camel-hair coat, but if the child was still there, Stella couldn't see her. The woman appeared not to see her either.

The bobble-jacket woman said, "You know, she was just here, running around. She's probably down the corridor."

The mother turned fiercely to reply. "She wouldn't run off. That wouldn't be like Maxie at all."

Stella privately felt that Maxie was exactly the sort of independent-minded kindergarten-aged child who ran off on her own: the sort of child that, in her experience, darted among the bushes at recess time while teachers coaxed them in firm tones back into the classroom. However, Maxie's mother no doubt knew her daughter. Her child was missing. This was a real problem that put Fairmount's mysteries in the shade.

It was not a crime. Not yet. And perhaps Stella could be of assistance. Forty years of dealing with little children like Maxie, along with her more recent experience investigating problems and crimes at Fairmount Manor, made her uniquely qualified to look into the little girl's disappearance.

"My child is missing." Maxie's mother sounded more worried still. She held out her arms towards the seated patients and visitors. "Can't you people look around you?"

Stella hurried towards Maxie's mother. Out of the corner of her eye she saw that despite a growing queue in front of the kiosk, the receptionist was also on the move, exiting her station, one palm raised to keep in place the waiting patients. Stella moved more quickly still in her good lace-up shoes (heaven knew how difficult those big bucket boots would be to walk in) to reach Maxie's mother before the receptionist could.

"I'll help you look." Stella squeezed Maxie's mom's arm comfortingly. "How old is your daughter? That will help us find her. That and her red hoodie."

"Maxie is only five years old."

"Oh my goodness, they're so adventurous at that age, aren't they?"

"Not Maxie."

"Of course," Stella murmured. But her sleuthing mind remembered the way Maxie had darted about, swift and bright, with a complete disregard for bumping into older persons on their chairs. Once again she recalled a top tenet of all investigations, which declared that most witnesses, including relatives, were entirely unreliable and sometimes even dishonest.

The receptionist approached. If Stella weren't so grateful to the receptionist for the information she'd given Stella regarding Thelma's likely whereabouts, she might have felt an even deeper chagrin at having her investigation interrupted so swiftly.

The receptionist looked from Stella to Maxie's mom. "Did I hear you say your child is missing?"

Maxie's mother covered her eyes. "I came to visit my Aunt Linda, but she was asleep. We were waiting, and now this happens …"

"We don't know that anything has happened, but we'll get on this immediately, of course. Where have you looked?"

"Just here." Maxie's mother covered her face with trembling hands. "Just around here. Maxie wouldn't go far."

"You haven't looked anywhere else?"

Maxie's mother shook her head behind her hands, and the receptionist directed an irritated look at Stella. Stella deduced from the glance that hospital receptionists held the same low regard for witnesses that sleuths did.

Stella said, "Maxie is wearing a red hoodie, and she's five."

"Oh, that kid. Sure. I remember her. I'll put out a heads-up on the address system. *Dr Dupray* is our code for a lost child. We take this very seriously. Maxie will be fine."

"Easy for you to say," Maxie's mom muttered.

Stella thanked the receptionist, who stepped smartly away back to her kiosk and picked up the phone. Despite the fact that all address systems broadcasts were difficult to grasp when one's ears were over eighty, Stella made out *Dr Dupray* and *red hoodie.*

The police officer strode back to reception, a few crumbs from his early lunch dotting his jacket breast. He strode past Stella and Maxie's mother to the sliding door and fiddled with an electrical box next to it, which, Stella supposed, locked the door. He pulled out a cell phone and spoke quietly into it.

Stella decided she could hardly have improved on the hospital's organization in the face of a sudden if uncertain emergency. In fact, she felt the same sort of satisfaction Hercule Poirot would have felt when Scotland Yard, despite its reluctance to cooperate with a private detective, covered the basics while he made the profound discoveries and deductions necessary to the case. She had noticed that a great difficulty with being a sleuth outside the legal system was getting the authorities to do one's bidding. But here stood the police officer, a little dozy perhaps after his sandwiches, but chock-full of authority and so big he would have made a good hockey goalie. Stella hoped the nurse appreciated his charms.

While the police officer locked down reception, Maxie's mother searched the far reaches of the area, beyond the seated patients. She peered around drinking water machines and under several tables spread with medical information booklets (*Dementia: What Can You Do About It?* caught Stella's eye) while patients and visitors stood to help her or twisted in their seats to watch her search. Stella followed Maxie's mother, thinking hard about the mystery of the child's disappearance. For, although it was likely that a simple search would turn up Maxie in whatever hidey-hole the child had crawled into, it was not a certainty. What if the child had been taken? What sort of a crime would this be?

That obvious worry came to mind, as it undoubtedly had occurred to everybody here. But Stella, as a career educator, was perfectly aware of the statistics regarding abductions by strangers. They were extremely rare. Furthermore, the obviously well-trained staff members searching the hospital (courtesy of *Dr Dupray*) were best placed to rescue Maxie if such were somehow the case. She considered the possible reasons for Maxie's disappearance.

1. Kidnapping for money was out of the question, for Maxie's mother was obviously not in funds. You only had to look at those seedy too-big bucket boots to know that.
2. However, the child might have been abducted by a family member, for example Maxie's estranged father, if such a person existed. Even so, why would a parent kidnap his own child in a hospital, of all well-staffed places? And the clincher against this possibility was that if there was the slightest chance of such a family-based crime, Maxie's mother would certainly be broadcasting it widely.

Either the child had left on her own, or she'd been taken somewhere by somebody. Stella tried to think of a third option but could not. Stella trailed Maxie's mother, who was now bent over, searching the waiting room at a knee-level view. She pulled back coats hanging on chairs and shoved handbags aside, peering under seating and between shoes. This was not a bad bit of searching. After all, the child was only five, and it was just possible that she'd curled up under one of the longer coats hanging there. She might even have fallen asleep. Maxie's mom crawled on the carpet and left handbags swinging as she passed, while patients and visitors stood up out of her way.

Stella stopped following Maxie's mother around the room. Instead she stood and studied the woman's progress. If Stella didn't know Maxie's mother was searching for her little daughter, she might have thought something rather different was going on. Witness that red handbag, expensive as all get out, swinging back and forth behind the camel-coated woman. It was not the only handbag hanging off the back of a visitor's chair. Stella walked closer to the camel-coated woman.

Yes, if Stella didn't know Maxie's mother was searching high and low—especially low—for her daughter, Stella might have thought the woman was rifling through handbags and maybe even coat pockets.

Maxie's mom returned to the centre of the room. Tearful and distraught, she turned towards the corridor leading to the café and elevators. And it was from this direction that her child's voice piped up, calling for her mother. The little girl in her Red-Riding hoodie skipped into reception. She held the pretty nurse by the hand, and at the sight, the police officer's face lit up as brightly as Maxie's mother's.

"There you are," Maxie's mother said.

"There I am," Maxie laughed.

"You're very naughty to run off. Come here."

Maxie ran to her mother, who took her in her arms. The child settled on her hip, looped an arm around her neck, and smiled around the room. The room smiled back.

Stella leaned down to the camel-coated woman. She murmured, "Better just check your handbag, don't you think?" She checked her own pockets for the wads of bills Vaughn had given her, and was reassured to find all as it should be.

The camel-coated woman looked sharply at Stella and reached for her bag. Several other visitors looked up and had obviously overheard; the advice would spread without any further input from her.

Stella approached Maxie's mom, Maxie, and the police officer.

She smiled at Maxie. "Just a little girl's hide-and-seek game, I'm relieved to see."

Maxie's mom shot her a frazzled glance. "I'm going to take this kid home and put her to bed."

"She says it," the little girl said, laughing, "but she doesn't mean it."

The police officer smiled at the pair. "I'm sure your mother will have a talk with you about running off."

He turned to open the door. Stella took the opportunity to look back and see how the women with their handbags were coming along. Several had pulled out wallets and were leafing through them. So wallets had not been taken. But then, where would the woman have concealed such bulky items?

Stella said to Maxie's mother, "But you haven't had your treatment yet?"

Maxie's mom frowned. "Treatment . . . ?"

"Not a treatment, then?"

The police officer pressed buttons and unfastened the door. It whisked open, and Maxie's mother thanked the police officer. "You say *thank you* too, Maxie."

Maxie, merry-eyed, did as she was asked.

Stella stepped between the woman and the doorway. "Or did you say you were here to visit somebody?"

"Aunt Lena, but she won't mind."

"Didn't you say Aunt *Linda*?" Stella smiled. "I probably got it wrong—my memory isn't my very best friend. Would you like me to give your aunt a message? What's her last name?"

"Don't bother, please. I'll phone her from— "

A wordless shout of discovery from the visitor's seating interrupted. The police officer turned to look.

The woman in the camel coat held up her wallet. "They're gone—they're not here."

"What's not here?" the police officer asked. "Is there another problem?"

Maxie's mom attempted to step through the door.

"It's always something, isn't it?" Stella stepped in front of Maxie's mother. "I'm so glad you're both all right, dear."

"Thank you so much." Maxie's mom sidestepped Stella.

Stella stepped back and had a little stumble. She held onto Maxie's mother's arm for balance.

The woman with the bobble jacket stood up. Her handbag hung open. "Mine is gone too."

"What's gone? Your wallet?"

"Not my wallet," the bobble jacket woman said.

"That woman took my credit cards," the camel-coated

woman said. "Maxie's mother. She was playing around with the handbags."

"I did not take anything." Maxie's mother attempted to remove Stella's hand, but Stella held on tight and tottered again for good measure.

"She took mine, too." The woman in the bobble jacket gazed around the seating area. "Everybody, check your bags and pockets."

Maxie's mother freed herself from Stella's grip, but by this time the police officer had the door shut and locked again. Maxie's mother set her child down on the entry mat and turned around to show no pockets in her bicycle pants and no handbag. "See? I haven't got anything."

"That's quite a trick to travel so lightly," Stella said. "Don't you have keys and licence for a car? And money for parking?"

"I have a bicycle. What's that got to do with anything?" Maxie's mom demanded.

"It's interesting, that's all. And may I say, good for you for saving the environment. But, heavens, where do you keep your bike lock keys?"

"It's a combination lock. May I go now?" Maxie's mother asked testily.

"In a minute." The police officer was nodding at a third woman, waving her wallet above her head. "You too, ma'am?"

"She was right behind me, flinging my coat around."

"I was looking for my child," Maxie's mom insisted. "You can see that I have nothing. Maxie, turn out your pockets."

Maxie did so. The police officer, Stella, and the rest of the room watched Maxie retrieve a cell phone, which she handed to her mother, and which the police officer took in his turn. Maxie pulled her empty pockets inside out and shook them.

Stella said, "You did that very well, Maxie. Not every five-year-old knows just how to turn out their pockets when asked, do they?"

"Not without some practice, I guess," the police officer said. He looked from Maxie to Maxie's mother, and to Maxie's mother's capacious bucket boots.

Stella followed his gaze. She said, "I don't think she'd be carrying anything in her boots, do you? She wasn't walking with a limp."

"Take off your boots," the police officer said.

Maxie's mother complied with rather good grace, Stella thought. The visitors and patients watched with increasing restlessness, and Stella overheard the receptionist calling security.

"See?" Maxie's mother shook her boots upside down. "Now are you satisfied? Please be good enough to open that door."

Stella stepped between the three of them and the door. "You might want to check those stretch pants. They're very tight, and I'm sure it's the sportive fashion, but, with apologies for my tactlessness, the padded backside could hide quite a few small flat items."

"Nothing shows." The police officer peered at the rear of the woman's stretch pants.

"Those are bicycle pants," Stella clarified. "They are tight, and they are padded. The cards wouldn't show, would they?"

Maxie's mother paled. Maxie took hold of her leg and stared at the four newly arriving, uniformed hospital personnel nearing the little group at reception's doorway. The camel-coated woman appeared intent on joining them, along with several others. Stella couldn't blame any of them for the intensity of their feelings: not Maxie's mother, or her victims, or the uniformed staff who would transition all of them into the legal system. Her own feelings were equally intense, if differently focussed. Mystery solved, she wished now to escape the drama and be out of the way before names were taken and statements required. And birth dates written down.

But escape would not be easy, for the women Maxie's mother had robbed assembled now around Stella like bridesmaids around a bride, if the bride wore a fleece warm-up suit.

The camel-coated woman and the woman with the bobble jacket hugged Stella. "You are certainly the smartest person here today."

The former nodded fiercely. "I would have been home before I noticed my cards missing if you hadn't spoken up."

"I'm so glad." Stella backed a step towards the door. "It's very nice of you to say so."

"Not at all ..."

"... we're in your debt."

Stella took another step towards the door. "Anybody would have done the same. I just happened to notice what was going on ..."

Laughter from all around Stella.

"... did you just happen to notice ...?"

"... *Observed,* that's what you did ..."

"... like some kind of detective ..."

"... lots more than the real police did ..."

This last came *sotto voce* from the camel-coated woman.

Sharon of the swollen ankles and Aunt Bethie reappeared in reception, eyes agog, and joined Stella's crew of admirers at the door.

"Did we miss some fun?" Sharon asked. "What happened when we were gone?"

The camel-coated woman said, "If you were here earlier, you

should check your bags to see if your credit cards are still in your wallet."

"Mine is," Bethie held out a brown waxed paper bag, a little spotted with oil or butter. "I just used it to buy Stella this. To say thank you for holding our place in line."

Stella took the bag. "How nice of you. What is it?"

Before Bethie could answer, the camel-coated woman brought the new arrivals up to date with the tale of Maxie's mother, Maxie, and the credit cards. The group watched the police officer enlist a female member of staff security to address the issue of the swag-concealing stretch bicycle pants. She put on disposable gloves. Without violating any laws of decency, she rescued several cards from their padded hiding place just below Maxie's mother's waist.

Maxie's mom snatched her cell phone back from the police officer. "I'm calling my lawyer."

"Your first good idea, miss. Ask him to meet us at the police station."

"You just keep your hands off my bum."

And at the word *bum,* Maxie giggled. Her laugh was so infectious that the robbery victims giggled too, along with the staff, police officer, Sharon, and Bethie. Stella sneaked another look at the door in time to see Riley's car tear up to the door and stop.

Stella murmured, "The clock strikes midnight, Cinderella." If Ollie had been here, he would have named her Cinder-Stella.

"What did you say?" Sharon asked.

"Just goodbye, and how much I enjoyed meeting you two. And thanks for this." Stella held up the paper bag Bethie had given her. She turned her back on the milling visitors, patients, staff, and Maxie and her criminal mom. The police officer opened the door for her, and as she passed through to the drive where Riley was lowering the window of his car, she felt no longer like an astronaut, but rather like an outer-space traveller leaving one world for another, blasting from the pull of civilization towards the heavier gravity of Fairmount Manor. She didn't want to put herself back into Riley's sphere of control. But where else could she go? Thelma was still in a hospital, which the receptionist had told her was very likely downtown, forty minutes' away with average traffic. She had to remove herself from the pull of hospital reception. Even then, Riley was not Stella's first choice for a chauffeur. *But needs must.* She finished the old saying to herself with a chuckle.

Just now he had one arm hanging out his window, and he was looking at her with disfavour.

She said, "Well, here you are. I guess you had to go quite a ways to find a gas station."

"Sure. Why aren't you inside? I said I'd meet you inside. We've got to get you checked in."

"Well, I'm feeling much better now."

"I'll need to find parking again. Get in. Next stop: Emergency."

"I'm completely myself again."

"That's beside the point. We'll do what we were told to do, you and I." He huffed an impatient breath.

Stella caught a hint of something in his tone, and then a hint of something else in his exhalation that had not been there before. Before she could be certain of its provenance, the reception door opened again and the accompanying rush of air dissipated the suspicious smell.

Sharon and Bethie stepped outside and joined her on the sidewalk beside Riley's car.

"Oh, good, we caught you," Sharon said. "That police officer wants to talk to you before you go."

"Police officer?" Riley stared from Sharon to Bethie, and then past them at reception's doors. "What happened with a police officer? What did you do, Mrs Ryman?"

Bethie said, "She didn't *do* anything. Is this your ride, Stella?"

Bethie and Sharon leaned close to the open driver's window to peer inside. Close enough that, when they pulled away, they exchanged a knowing look.

Sharon said, "Stella's a heroine, actually. Come and talk to the police officer."

Stella said, "I don't think I need to— "

"No she doesn't," Riley said, but he said it to the backs of the two women who were hurrying off back into reception. Sharon had a hand raised towards the police officer.

Stella leaned closer to see whether she had or had not imagined the new odour emanating from Riley.

Riley said, "Please, Mrs Ryman, get into the car and let me take you to Emergency."

"Just a minute, please." Stella had not, after all, imagined it. And now, having smelled what she smelled, she would not need to convince him, trick him, or trap him into helping her. She could just blackmail him. What a relief. She said, "I have somewhere else I'd like you to drive me now."

"Excuse me?" Riley put his head out the window. "I'm not driving you anywhere except Emergency—and then back to Fairmount when the doctors are finished with you."

"You've been to the pub, haven't you?"

"For a sandwich and coffee ..." His eyebrows rose, which body language Stella recognized: it meant that he was telling a lie. In this case, a lie of omission.

She said, "And beer. More than one, I'd guess, from your breath."

"I haven't."

"You have. Don't argue. It's as plain on you as if you'd painted your nose purple. Are you able to drive properly?"

"Of course I am."

Stella nodded. "Well, I'll have to take your word for it."

"Thanks for nothing, Mrs Ryman."

"You're equally welcome, Riley. Now, let's not fight. I need you to drive me downtown."

The door behind them opened again, and this time Sharon and Bethie had the police officer between them.

The police officer said, "Mrs Ryman, I appreciate your help with those credit card robberies. Good observation, well done."

"*Help* is hardly the word," Sharon said. "Stella solved the whole thing for you. Maxie's mother must be playing that little scam in waiting rooms all around town."

"Stella gave you the thief on a plate," Bethie added.

"I *said* thank you. Now, Mrs Ryman, I want a word with your driver." The policeman walked over to Riley's car. Sharon and Bethie stood next to Stella with their arms crossed, and the look they gave Riley was anything but pleasant.

The police officer said, "Please get out of the car, sir."

Riley said, "Damn."

The police officer opened the driver's door, and Riley climbed out. He didn't look at Stella or the two women beside her. He looked at the sidewalk, as if he were measuring it for a drunk test.

"Did you drive here, sir?" the police officer asked.

There was no other way he could have arrived on the scene in his car. Riley sighed and nodded.

"I'll have to ask you to come with me," the police officer told him. "You'll take a breathalyzer."

Riley said, "But what about my passenger? I have to take Mrs Ryman to Emergency."

Sharon spoke up. "You're not taking Stella anywhere, you day-drinker driver. Here's where you get towed."

Riley gestured to the car. "This is a classic Saab. Let me take off the brake, or you'll wreck it if you tow it."

"I'm sure Mrs Ryman can drive it for you," the police officer said.

"That's a fine idea," Bethie said. "You don't need this fellow at all, Stella. Imagine him offering you a ride and then drinking beers."

Sharon said, "There are laws about that, I think."

Riley said, "Mrs Ryman can't drive."

Now it came.

"She's over eighty and demented. Although not as demented as some," he added, in an apparent attempt to be fair. "She lives in Fairmount Care Home. She can't be out on her own."

Bethie said, "What a crock. She's sixty-nine."

"What?" Riley said. "She's not. She's *never.*"

"She totally is. You're so obviously over the limit, guy." Sharon turned to the police officer. "He's not allowed to drive Stella anywhere, is he?"

"Not in his condition. He can wait inside with the credit card thief."

"You're all nuts. I wash my hands." Riley let the police officer lead him away.

Bethie opened the car door for Stella. Sharon handed her a business card. "Call us some time, won't you?"

Bethie nodded at the paper bag in Stella's hand. "And have a good lunch."

"But don't eat and drive," Sharon joked.

Stella climbed into the driver's seat of Riley's old Saab and set the bag Bethie had given her down on the passenger seat beside her. She had always driven standard—it had been a point of pride with her throughout her life to drive only standard cars—but today she was not unhappy to see that Riley's car was an automatic. She had three bridges to drive over in order to reach downtown, and honestly she'd never thought to be behind the wheel of a car again.

Soldier on, Stella.

Stella imagined Thelma, all alone in a hospital bed, her small body pressed nearly flat by heavy white sheets folded back at her neck. Thelma, tiny and fragile, hot in temper. She would be terrified that she would leave the hospital with her hip repaired—but feet first in her red silk slippers, deceased and soon forgotten by the world outside Fairmount, if not by her friends there.

Stella adjusted the rear-view mirror of Riley's Saab. A police car pulled up just behind her, warning lights flashing. Two police officers climbed out of their vehicle and entered the hospital. Stella saw the handcuffs clipped to their back pockets, shiny and circular, like odd kitchen gadgets that measured, perhaps, large servings of spaghetti. She looked up through the driver's window at Sharon and Bethie and returned their farewell waves. Inside reception, a small crowd milled around Maxie's mother, Riley, and the police officers that had joined the group. What a flurry of justice she'd helped to loose upon the hospital. She should have felt victory, or possibly guilt. But she did not, for it was all in a day's work for an amateur sleuth.

Now. *Hang on, Thelma. I'm coming.*

She checked her side mirror and reached down for the lever that pulled her seat closer to the steering wheel. It was all coming back to her now.

She touched her brake with an experimental toe and moved the transmission to drive.

THE ARTISTS

Claire Lawrence

Cover artist, Dreaming Underwater

Claire Lawrence is a storyteller and visual artist living in British Columbia, Canada. Her writing has been published and won fiction and nonfiction awards in Canada and worldwide, and has been nominated for a Pushcart Prize. Her artwork has appeared in publications including *Inverted Syntax, Gone Lawn, Auxocardia, Coffin Bell, Intima: A Journal on Narrative Medicine,* and *3Elements.* In 2021, her artwork was nominated for *Best of the Net.* Claire's goal is to publish in all genres and not inhale too many fumes. You can find her short story 'Life Supports' in *Pulp Literature* Issue 30, Spring 2021.

Dreaming Underwater is an original acrylic and alcohol ink on Yupo paper. This piece is for those who identify as women and are embroiled in facing nightmares, fighting demons, enduring emotional scars, or living in abusive or unsustainable conditions: you are strong, smart, resilient. You are enough. Wake and rise.

Matthew Nielsen

Illustrator, 'Then and Now: An ASD Comic'

Matthew Nielsen is a British-Canadian illustrator. He has had the honour of working on commissions for Monstercat, Imperiad Entertainment, Military History Visualized, and others. He was diagnosed with Asperger's Syndrome at age eleven. With encouragement and advice from his friends, Matthew has been able to write this short comic about his experiences growing up and living with autism. He's considering writing a graphic novel about it someday. In the meantime he's honing his skills (both artistically and socially).

If you're looking for even more to read, he always has a long list of graphic novel recommendations. He hopes to one day be able to work as an illustrator for a living, and rise up to the challenge of providing people with excellent artwork. So long as he enjoys it, he'll keep at it. Find out more about his work at nuclearjackal.com, on Instagram and Twitter @nuclearjackal, or read his comics at tapas.io/NuclearJackal/series.

Mel Anastasiou
In-house illustrator
Mel Anastasiou loves drawing for *Pulp Literature* because she loves the stories she illustrates. She draws in black and white, working from imagination and inspired by details from Renaissance compositions. You can find illustrations, writing tips, and news about her books and novellas at melanastasiou.wordpress.com, and see more of her artwork on Facebook at Bird and Branch Artwork.

HALL OF FAME

These are the heroes—the Patrons and Pulp Literati whose monthly support helped bring you this issue. Please lift your glasses and give them a rousing cheer!

The Brewers
Robin McGillveray

The Landlords
Isabel Cushey
Dana Tye Rally
Adam Fout

The Innkeepers
Ada Maria Soto
Margot Landels
Ev Bishop
Susan Jackson
Kevin Harris
Gillian Gardiner
Richard Ohnemus
Lorna Erns

The Cicerones
Roger & Anne Anastasiou
Carol Tulpar

The Bartenders
Alana Krider
Richard Gropp
Ron Graves
Dave Wayne
Scott F Gray
Michelle Balfour
Abigail Bruce
Vernice Dietra Malik
Katriona Greenmoor
AD Bane
KT Wagner
Deepthi Atukorala
Margot Spronk
Margaret Elliott
Peter Halasz
Bjarne Hansen
Leny Wagner
Kain Stewart
Chris Olee
kc dyer
Kimberley Aslett
Brighton Hugg
Alexa Benzaid-Williams
Bryan Moose
Maureen Cooke
K Anastasiou
Mike Sylvester
Katherine Derbyshire
Rapscallion
Shannon Saunders
Megan Shaw
James Carlino
Benjamin Johnson
Suzanne Philip
Lin & John Richardson
Jennifer Getsinger
Finnian Burnett

The Regulars
Marta Salek
Rina Piccolo
Jenny Blackford
Akemi Art
BC
Meredith Frazier
Catherine Levinson
Vera
Charity Tahmaseb
Marilyn Holt
Barbara Pengelly
David Perlmutter
Steve Mashburn
Hannah McManus
Paul Anguiano

If you would like to join the ranks of these worthies, you can become a patron on Patreon at patreon.com/pulplit or join the Pulp Literati through our website at pulpliterature.com/join-pulp-literati/.

LUH 63A

MARKETPLACE

Books

Advent *by Michael Kamakana* • We thought we knew what the aliens wanted. Think again. • pulpliterature.com/advent

Allaigna's Song: Chorale *by JM Landels* The long-awaited conclusion to the bestselling *Allaigna's Song* trilogy. • pulpliterature.com/allaignas-song

The Extra: A Monument Studios Mystery *by Mel Anastasiou* • Extra Frankie Ray gets her big break on the Silver Screen, until Murder steals the scene. • pulpliterature.com/the-extra

The Labours of Mrs Stella Ryman: Further Fairmount Mysteries *by Mel Anastasiou* • Trapped in a down-at-the-heels care home. You'd be cranky too. • pulpliterature.com/stella-ryman-and-the-fairmount-manor-mysteries

What the Wind Brings *by Matthew Hughes* • Winner of the 2020 Endeavour Award • pulpliterature.com/product-category/novels/matthew-hughes

The Writer's Boon Companion *by Mel Anastasiou* • Thirty Days Towards an Extraordinary Volume • pulpliterature.com/subscribe/the-bookstore

Bookstores

Russell Books • 100-747 Fort St, Victoria, BC • russellbooks.com

Western Sky Books • 2132-2850 Shaughnessy St, Port Coquitlam, BC V3C 6K5 • 604-461-5602 • store.westernskybooks.com

White Dwarf / Dead Write Books • 3715 10th Ave W, Vancouver, BC V6R 2G5 • 604-228-8223 • whitedwarf@deadwrite.com

Conferences & Events

When Words Collide • August 4–6, 2023 Calgary, AB • whenwordscollide.org

Wine Country Writers' Festival • September 2023 • winecountrywriters-festival.ca

Surrey International Writers' Conference October 2023 • siwc.ca

Writing Resources

Dreamers Creative Writing • Workshops, residencies, contests & more! • www.dreamerswriting.com

Quit the Day Job • A school for writers from Pulp Literature Press pulpliterature.com/quit-the-day-job

The Writers' Lodge on Bowen Island The Muse retreats for writers • pulpliterature.com/calendar-of-events/retreats/

Magazines

Amazing Stories · Back in print! amazingstories.com

The Digest Enthusiast · Digests past & present plus new genre fiction larquepress.com

EVENT Magazine · Poetry & prose eventmagazine.ca

Geist · Ideas + Culture · Made in Canada · geist.com

Mystery Weekly Magazine · The cutting edge of short mystery fiction www.mysteryweekly.com

Neo-opsis · Canadian magazine of science fiction based in Victoria, BC · neo-opsis.ca

OnSpec · The Canadian magazine of the fantastic · onspecmag.wordpress.com

Polar Borealis · Paying market for new Canadian SF&F writers & artists · polarborealis.ca

Room Magazine · Literature, Art & Feminism since 1975 · roommagazine.com

Printing & Publishing

First Choice Books/Victoria Bindery Book printing & binding · graphic design · eBooks · marketing materials 1-800-957-0561 · firstchoicebooks.ca

CONTESTS

Pulp Literature runs four annual contests for poetry, flash fiction, and short stories. For contest guidelines, prizes, and entry fees, see pulpliterature.com/contests.

The Raven Short Story Contest
Contest opens: 1 September 2023
Deadline: 15 October 2023
Winner notified: 15 November 2023
Winner published: Issue 42, Spring 2024
Prize: $300

The Bumblebee Flash Fiction Contest
Contest opens: 1 January 2024
Deadline: 15 February 2024
Winner notified: 15 March 2024
Winner published: Issue 43, Summer 2024
Prize: $300

The Magpie Award for Poetry
Contest opens: 1 March 2023
Deadline: 15 April 2023
Winner notified: 15 May 2023
Winner published: Issue 44, Autumn 2024
Prize: $500

The Hummingbird Flash Fiction Prize
Contest opens: 1 May 2024
Deadline: 15 June 2024
Winner notified: 15 July 2024
Winner published: Issue 45, Winter 2025
Prize: $300

Become a Patron of Pulp Literature

By supporting ***Pulp Literature*** on Patreon with $2 or more per month, you will be laying the foundation for a secure future for the magazine, as well as ensuring that you never miss an issue! Your subscription includes four big issues of short stories, novellas, poetry, comics, and novel excerpts, delivered to your door or electronic mailbox each year. **Find us at patreon.com/pulplit**

If you prefer to subscribe through our website, go to pulpliterature.com/subscribe.

Or you can send a cheque with the form below to
Subscriptions, Pulp Literature Press, 21955 16 Ave, Langley BC, V2Z 1K5, Canada

Don't miss an issue!

- ❑ **Send me 2 years (8 issues) at the special rate of $90** (save $30)*
- ❑ **Send me 1 year (4 issues) for $50** (save $10)*
- ❑ **Send me 2 years of digital issues for $30** (save $9.92)
- ❑ **Send me 1 year of digital issues for $17.50** (save $2.47)

Name: ______________________________
Address: ______________________________
City: ____________________ Prov. / State: __________
Postal code: __________ Country: ____________________
Email: ______________________________

- ❑ Payment enclosed
- ❑ Bill me
- ❑ New
- ❑ Renewal

Make cheques payable in Canadian funds to Pulp Literature Press. Include email address for digital editions and Paypal billing, or subscribe at www.pulpliterature.com.

*for postage outside Canada add $20 per year in North America or $36 per year overseas.

www.ingramcontent.com/pod-product-compliance
Lightning Source LLC
Chambersburg PA
CBHW070352200726
48294CB00003B/867

* 9 7 8 1 9 8 8 8 6 5 5 7 7 *